"I found her in the snowstorm," said Bert.

The Bobbsey Twins Keeping House

BY

LAURA LEE HOPE

AUTHOR OF "THE BOBBSEY TWIN SERIES."

NEW YORK
GROSSET & DUNLAP
PUBLISHERS

Made in the United States of America

CONTENTS

THE BOBBSEY TWINS
KEEPING HOUSE

CHAPTER I

DOWN IN A PIPE

"Now it's Freddie's turn!" called Nan
Bobbsey. "Get ready to catch the ball," and
she motioned, showing that she was going to
toss it to her small brother.

"No, I want to have it once more!" cried
Flossie, who was Freddie's twin sister. "Come
on, Nan! Please throw it to me!" and she
jumped up and down, her light, fluffy hair
tossing about her head. It was cold out in
the yard where the children were playing, and
that is one reason why Flossie jumped up and
down. Another reason was that she was excited about the ball game Nan had gotten up
for the smaller twins. "Come on, toss it to
me!" begged Flossie.

"But it isn't your turn, dear!" objected Nan. "It's Freddie's turn. He wants to catch, too," and she held the big rubber ball, looking at Flossie meanwhile.

"Oh, just one more turn for me!" Flossie begged, jumping up and down faster than ever.

"Oh, all right! Let her have it!" agreed Freddie, good-naturedly. "I'll wait."

"That's kind of you," said Nan. "All right, Flossie, you may have this next toss! Get ready!"

"One more turn for me!" sang Flossie gaily. "One more turn for me! Hurry up, Nan, please!"

Flossie stopped her jumping-jack movements, and with outstretched hands and shining eyes awaited the ball, which Nan tossed across an old flower bed. In the past summer bright blossoms had made this part of the garden very gay. But now, with winter coming on, the flowers had been killed by Jack Frost and the stalks were sear and brown.

"I got it!" cried Flossie. But she spoke a

moment too soon, for the ball just touched the tips of her fingers, bounced off, and rolled across the frozen ground of the flower garden right to Freddie's feet. He picked it up.

"Oh, dear!" sighed Flossie. She had so much wanted to catch the ball this last time, but she had missed it.

"You muffed!" cried Freddie. He had heard his older brother Bert speak like that when, in a real ball game, some boy failed to hold the ball. "You muffed it, Flossie!"

Then, seeing that there were tears in his twin sister's eyes, Freddie did a very manly and generous thing.

"You can have another turn," he said. "Toss it to Flossie again, Nan. I don't mind waiting."

"That's nice of you, Freddie," said Nan.

"Thank you!" cried Flossie, quickly "squeezing back" her tears. "I'll give you some of my candy, Freddie!"

"Will you?" he exclaimed. "What kind is it, Flossie?"

"It isn't any kind yet, 'cause I haven't got it," the little golden-haired girl explained as

Nan took the ball from her small brother and got ready to throw it again. "But I mean when I do get some candy I'll give you a piece."

"Oh!" exclaimed Freddie, somewhat disappointed. "Well, anyhow, you can have another turn to catch the ball."

"Maybe if Nan should take us down town now she would buy us some candy," went on Flossie, getting ready for this next attempt to catch the rubber ball. "Then I could give you some, Freddie."

"Ho! Ho!" laughed Nan. "That's a gentle hint, I suppose, Flossie, for me to take you after candy. But I'm afraid I can't to-day. Now get ready. If you miss the ball this time it won't be fair to make Freddie wait any longer."

"I'll catch it this time!" cried Flossie, and she did. Right in her hands she caught the bouncing rubber, and then she threw it back to Nan while Freddie got ready for his turns.

Meanwhile, Flossie danced about, waiting until the ball would again come to her. Flossie was a lively little girl—always dancing, running, singing, or doing something. And Freddie was about the same. In fact, the Bobbsey twins were a lively set of youngsters.

Freddie had caught the ball four times and Nan was getting ready to toss it to him for the fifth when a whistle was heard around the corner of the house.

"Here comes Bert!" cried Flossie, and she darted off to meet her older brother. Bert was Nan's twin and these two were a few years older than the smaller Bobbsey twins.

"Maybe Bert will want to play ball," suggested Freddie, as he caught the rubber sphere for the fifth time, making a perfect score for him.

"We'll see," replied Nan.

But when Bert came whistling around the corner of the house, Flossie holding him by one hand. he seemed to have something else in mind than playing toss-ball with his smaller brother and sister.

"You can't guess what I know!" he called,

swinging Flossie around in a circle by her two hands, her feet flying off the ground.

"Have you got candy?" the little girl demanded, when Bert had set her down.

"Candy? No!" he laughed. "But there's a new horse in our garage."

"A horse in our garage!" cried Nan. "Do you mean a runaway?"

"No, he isn't running away—he's just standing there," Bert answered, with a grin.

"How did a horse get in our garage?" asked Flossie.

"A man put it there," Bert answered.

"Oh, I don't believe you!" exclaimed Nan.

"A horse couldn't get in our garage!" added Freddie.

"Why not?" Bert wanted to know. "It's big enough—our garage is. And, anyhow, it used to be a stable with horses in it before daddy made it over for automobiles. Of course a horse could be in our garage."

"Well, maybe it could," admitted Nan. "But what's the horse doing there?"

"Just standing still."

"Is he eating?" Flossie wanted to know.

Bert thought this over for a moment before he answered:

"No, the horse isn't eating."

There was something in her brother's voice that made Nan look at him sharply. Then she cried:

"Look here, Bert Bobbsey, there's something queer about this! What kind of a horse is it?"

Before Bert could answer Freddie asked:

"Has the horse four legs?"

"Yes, indeed, it has four legs! I'm sure of that for I just counted them!" and Bert seemed so very positive on this point that Nan didn't know what to think.

"Come on and I'll show you the horse if you don't believe me," offered Bert, moving off toward the garage.

All thoughts of keeping on with the ball game were now forgotten by Flossie and Freddie. They were eager to see the strange horse in their father's garage. Nan could not imagine how the animal could have been put there.

"But maybe one of the store wagons broke

and they had to leave the horse in our garage until they get the wagon fixed," she thought to herself.

Into the garage ran the Bobbsey twins, Flossie and Freddie merrily laughing, Bert with a queer look on his face, and Nan ready for almost anything.

"Where's the horse?" demanded Freddie, entering first and looking around.

"I don't see any horse," added Flossie, who had closely followed her small brother.

"There it is!" exclaimed Bert.

He pointed to a carpenter's sawhorse in one corner of the building.

For a moment the smaller children looked at it in surprise. Then Freddie burst out laughing.

"Oh, ho! A sawhorse! A sawhorse!" he exclaimed.

"But it has got four legs—one, two, three, four!" counted Flossie. "Oh, isn't it funny! I thought you meant a real horse, Bert."

"So did I!" said Freddie.

"And I did, too, for a little while," admitted Nan. "But pretty soon I thought it must be a joke. And I don't think it's a very good joke, either, Bert Bobbsey, so there!"

"Well, let's see you think of a better joke!" laughed Nan's twin brother. "Ha! Ha! I had you all fooled! It's a sawhorse, and you all thought it was a real horse! Oh, ho!"

"I can get on the back of this sawhorse," announced Freddie. "Look at me!" He ran toward the wooden thing.

"Don't fall!" cautioned Nan. But this Freddie almost did in climbing up on the sawhorse, which was rather a high one. Bert caught him just in time.

"How did it get here?" Freddie asked, when he was seated on the back of the "animal."

"The carpenters have been working here, and they left it," Bert explained. "When I saw it I thought it would be a good joke to make believe it was a real horse. And I fooled all of you!"

Nan was going to say again that she had not been fooled very much when Flossie, looking out of the window, cried:

"Oh, it's snowing! It's snowing!"

"Is it? Really?" Freddie wanted to know. "Are you fooling like Bert was with the saw-horse, Flossie?"

"No, it's really snowing!" the little girl answered.

"Oh, hurray! I want to see it!" cried Freddie, and he was in such a hurry to descend from the back of the sawhorse that this time he fell in real earnest. However, as there was a pile of shavings on the floor, left there by the carpenters, Freddie fell into them and was not hurt at all. But he was covered with the shavings.

However, Nan picked him up and brushed him off, and then he ran to the window out of which the others were looking.

"It really is snowing!" said Nan.

"Looks as if it would last, too," added Bert.

"Oh, can I have my sled out?" begged Flossie.

"I want mine, too!" chimed in Freddie. "Oh, I'm so glad it's winter and we're going to have ice and snow! Come on, let's go sleigh-riding! Hurray!"

"Don't be in such a rush," advised Bert.

"There'll have to be more snow than this before you can use your sleds."

"But quite a lot has fallen, and it's still snowing hard," said Nan. "It must have started soon after we came in here."

The twins had been in the garage some little time, laughing and talking about Bert's joke and playing on the carpenter's sawhorse, and in that period the ground had been whitened with the flurry of flakes.

"I'm going out and see how deep it is," announced Freddie.

Before either Nan or Bert could stop him, if they had wanted to, the little fellow went to a side door of the garage and, opening this, rushed out. But he did not go far.

Right at the door a new drain was being put in. A large sewer pipe was set upright in the ground. Work around it was not yet finished, and that was why the side door had been closed.

But Freddie opened it. Then he slipped on the newly fallen snow and a moment later disappeared down the drain pipe!

CHAPTER II

A BROKEN WINDOW

FOR a moment following Freddie's accident there was silence. Even the little fellow
himself was so frightened that he forgot to
cry out. But a second or two later he found
his voice and set up a series of yells.

"Oh! Oh! Get me out! Help me,
Bert!" he begged.

"Oh, Freddie, you poor boy!" gasped Nan.

"Is he dead? Will we ever get him up?"
Flossie wanted to know, and she burst into
tears.

"Yes! Yes! I'll get him out! He can't
fall any farther!" shouted Bert. "I'll lift
him out in a minute! You're all right, Freddie," he went on. "Don't cry any more!"

"I am *not* all right!" wailed the little chap.
"I'm down in a pipe! How can I—be all—
all right—when I'm in a pipe?"

He was crying and Flossie was sobbing.
Nan did not know what to do.

Bert, however, seemed to know what he
was about. He hurried to the edge of the
drain pipe, down which his small brother had
slipped, and began to consider the best way
to get Freddie out.

And while Bert is doing that I shall take
just a moment to tell my new readers something about the four children. They were
first introduced to you in the book called
"The Bobbsey Twins," and in that you read
about Mr. Richard Bobbsey and his wife,
Mary, who lived in the eastern city of Lakeport on Lake Metoka. Mr. Bobbsey owned
a lumberyard there.

There were two sets of twins. Bert and
Nan were the older. They had dark brown
hair and brown eyes. Flossie and Freddie
had light hair and blue eyes. Thus the
Bobbsey twins were quite a contrast, and
when the four walked down the street together more than one person turned to look
at them.

The children had good times and many

adventures. They went to the country, to the seashore, and of course attended school. Once they visited Snow Lodge and were storm-bound. They had traveled on the deep blue sea, gone out West, spent some time in Cedar Camp, and had gone through some exciting times at a county fair. They had also camped out.

The book just before this one is called "The Bobbsey Twins and Baby May," and tells how they found a strange little baby and what happened to it.

Now winter was coming on again, and the children counted on having more fun. Bert had played his joke about the sawhorse, and then had followed Freddie's fall down the drain pipe.

"Can you get him up?" asked Nan anxiously.

"Sure I can!" Bert answered. "You stand over there, Nan, on the other side of him. Reach down in the pipe and put your hand under Freddie's left arm."

Nan did this while Bert did the same thing on the other side. The drain pipe was about

as large as Freddie's body. He had slid into
it feet first, and his hands were down at his
sides. The pipe was not large enough for
him to lift his hands over the edge, or he
might have pushed himself out.

But with Bert and Nan to lift him, he was
soon pulled from the drain, more vexed than
hurt. Though it was found later that he had
skinned one shin rather painfully.

"There you are!" cried Bert, as he and Nan
set their little brother on his feet out on the
snow-covered ground. "You are all right,
Freddie. And don't go jumping down any
more pipes!"

"I didn't jump down!" declared the little
fellow, with some indignation. "I slipped
in!"

"You went in so quick," observed Flossie,
"it was as if the sawhorse kicked you in,
wasn't it, Freddie?"

"Yes, it was," he said, and then he laughed.
So did Bert and Nan. A moment later, however, a look of pain passed over Freddie's face
and he put one hand down on his left shin.

"What's the matter?" Nan asked.

"My leg hurts!"

"Maybe it's broken," suggested Flossie.

"How could I walk if my leg was broken?" the little boy demanded, and he strutted about, though he limped a little.

"Let me look," suggested Bert, and when he had pulled down Freddie's stocking they all saw that the shin had been skinned and was bleeding slightly. It had been scraped on the edge of the drain pipe.

"Oh, look!" cried Flossie. "He's got the nose bleed on his leg!"

Freddie had been going to cry at the sight of the blood. But when Flossie said this in such a funny way he laughed, and so did Bert and Nan.

"We'd better take him in the house and fix his leg," said Bert to his twin.

"Yes," Nan agreed.

"Can't I go sleigh-riding?" Freddie wanted to know. "Look how nice it's snowing!"

The white flakes were, indeed, swirling down faster than ever. For the first snow of the season, it was quite a storm, and the ground was now covered with the soft flakes.

"Oh, my dear, what has happened?" cried Mrs. Bobbsey, when she saw Freddie, covered with snow, limping toward the house, escorted by Nan, Bert and Flossie.

"I—I fell in a pipe!" Freddie answered.

"A *pipe?* What sort of game were you playing?" his mother wanted to know.

"It wasn't a game," said Bert, and then he explained.

Freddie's leg felt better after his mother had bandaged it with some soothing salve, and then he was allowed to go out and play in the snow on his sled with Flossie.

Bert had thought the snow would not amount to much, but a little later he, too, got out his sled.

Nan did likewise, and the Bobbsey twins and some of their friends had a jolly time on a little coasting hill not far from the house.

"Winter's come pretty early this year," said Charlie Mason, one of Bert's chums, as the two boys went down the hill together, bobsled fashion.

"Yes," agreed Bert. "We'll have a lot of fun at school to-morrow, making a snow fort. That is, if the snow doesn't melt."

But there was plenty of snow on the ground when the children awakened the next morning, though the storm had stopped and the sun was shining.

"I hope the sun doesn't melt all the snow," sighed Flossie, as she got ready to accompany her twin brother to school. They were in a lower class than Bert and Nan, but the smaller twins generally walked along with the older brother or sister.

It was when the Bobbsey twins were almost at school that John Marsh, a boy of about Bert's age, came running around the corner of the street. John seemed rather out of breath and excited.

"What's the matter?" asked Bert.

"Oh, that Danny Rugg and Sam Todd are pegging snowballs at me," said John. "I wouldn't mind soft ones, but they're using hard balls. And they're two to one—Sam and Danny both pegged at me."

"That isn't fair!" cried Bert. "They

ought to fight square—even on both sides—
and with soft balls. Come on, I'll help
you!"

Together the two lads went back and
around the corner to the street where Danny
and his rather mischievous crony were standing, leaving Nan to go with Flossie and Freddie on to school.

"Hi! There's John again!" yelled Sam
Todd, as he caught sight of the boy who had
run away.

"Soak him!" shouted Danny Rugg.

But a moment later the two little bullies,
for that is what they were, caught sight of
Bert Bobbsey with John and the hands they
had raised to throw the hard snowballs fell
back at their sides.

"Hello, Danny!" called Bert, for they were
on somewhat friendly terms.

"Hello," said Danny, not very cheerfully.

"Do you want to snowball fight?" demanded Sam Todd.

"No, not now," Bert answered. "But, anyhow, when you do fight you ought to use soft
balls. and not two of you fellows go for one."

"We didn't use hard balls!" Danny declared.

"You did so!" cried John. "And you both pegged at me at once!"

"Aw, well, it was only in fun," grumbled Danny. Now that Bert had joined John the odds were against the bullies, for Sam Todd was not a very large lad. "We'll fight you after school if you like," went on Danny. "Hard balls or soft balls, and the same number on each side."

"And we'll lick you, too!" boasted Sam.

"We'll see about that!" laughed Bert. "I don't know if I want a snowball fight or not. But I'm not going to throw any now, I know that. It's too near the school," for the boys had been walking along as they talked.

"We aren't within a block yet," declared Danny. "It's only against the rule to throw snowballs within a block of the school," and he rounded in his hands a ball he had been making.

"I'm not scared to throw one now," declared Sam, and he tossed a ball at a signboard, hitting it a resounding whack.

"Neither am I!" exclaimed Danny, and he also threw. As he did so Bert and John saw something on Danny's finger gleaming golden in the sun. The flash seemed to remind Danny of an important matter, for he held up his right hand and cried: "Look at that! Isn't that a peach? It's a new gold ring I got for my birthday."

"You're lucky," remarked Bert, as Danny held the ring out to be admired.

"I guess I am," boasted Danny. "No fellow in our school has a valuable gold ring like that! My father gave it to me."

"I should think you wouldn't like to wear it for fear you might lose it," remarked John.

"Naw, I won't lose it," drawled Danny. "Go on, Bert!" he cried. "I dare you to throw a snowball at the signboard. You can't throw as straight as I did!"

"Yes, I can!" said Bert, who did not like this said of him.

"Go on! Let's see you!" cried Sam Todd.

As the lads were still more than a block away from the school, they could, without breaking the rule, throw snowballs.

Accordingly, Bert and John tossed a few, and Bert made much better shots than did either Danny or Sam, though John did not do so well.

"That's because I ran and got out of breath when you two were pegging hard balls at me," he said to the two bullies.

"Aw, we were only in fun," Danny said.

"Two to one isn't fair, though," cried Bert.

"Well, you're two now—do you want to fight?" asked Sam, who seemed eager for a battle in the snow.

Before Bert or John could answer the clanging of a bell sounded on the clear, frosty air, and Nan Bobbsey, who came through a side street with Flossie and Freddie, cried:

"That's the next to the last bell! You'd better hurry if you don't want to be late, Bert!"

"All right, I'm hurrying," he said.

Even Danny Rugg, bold as he sometimes was, did not seem inclined to break the school rule and throw balls within the block limit set by Mr. Tarton, the principal. However, he still held one of the white missiles in his hand. This he tossed up and down, catching it before it had time to reach the ground. Danny's new, gold birthday ring sparkled in the sun.

"Let me wear that ring of yours sometime, will you, Danny?" asked Sam, as he walked on beside his crony.

"Maybe," was the answer.

"And if Bert and his crowd want to have a snowball fight after school," went on Sam in a low voice, "I know where I can find a lot of horse chestnuts."

"What good'll horse-chestnuts be in a snowball fight?" Danny wanted to know.

Sam looked around to make sure no one would hear him, then he said:

· "We can put a horse-chestnut inside a soft snowball and make it sting like anything when it hits! I can get a lot of 'em. Shall I?"

"Maybe," agreed Danny. He was a bully, but not quite as mischievous as was Sam.

On toward the school hurried the boys and girls. The echoes of the next to the last bell were ringing in their ears.

"Better get rid of our snowballs, I guess," said Bert to John, as they crossed the street which would put them within one block of the school. "Mr. Tarton might see us."

"That's right," agreed John. "Chuck your balls away, fellows!" he called. "We're within a block." He got rid of his own sphere of snow and Bert tossed his to one side. Several of the other boys who were near did likewise.

Then, suddenly, there was a crash of glass and the pupils looking up in startled amazement, saw that a snowball had gone through one of the beautiful stained-glass windows in a church near the school. A large piece was broken out from the window picture.

"Oh! Oh!" yelled many voices.

"Who broke the window?" cried the girls and boys.

Then, as the last bell began to ring, they all began to run so they would not be late.

CHAPTER III

THE LOST RING

INTO the lower halls and corridors of the school poured the children. The last bell was still clanging, and they would not be marked late if they reached their classrooms before the last peal. The bell would ring for several minutes yet.

On all sides, as the boys and girls hurried in, could be heard talks and gasps of astonishment, not unmixed with fear, about the breaking of the church window.

"Oh, did you see it?"

"Did you hear it?"

"Didn't it make a big crash!"

"What'll the church people say?"

"I guess that window must 'a' cost a thousand dollars!"

"Who did it?"

This last question was the one most often asked.

But no one seemed to know, or, if any one did, he or she was not telling about it. Nan hurried with Flossie and Freddie to their classroom, and then she hastened back toward her own. Bert was in Nan's room, and, seeing her brother just before she entered the door, Nan whispered:

"Bert, did you break the church window?"

"No," he answered, "I didn't. Of course I didn't do it!"

"Do you know who did it?"

Bert did not answer for a second or two. For the moment he and Nan were by themselves, just outside their classroom door. Then Bert looked down the corridor and saw Danny Rugg and Sam Todd coming along.

"Do you know who did it?" repeated Nan.

"Maybe I do," Bert answered slowly. "And maybe I don't," he added, as Nan gave a gasp of surprise. "Anyhow, I'm not going to tell."

That was all there was time to say. The last bell was giving its final strokes, and Bert and his sister hurried to their seats. Danny and Sam, with other boys and girls, also hastened in to their room; and then came silence, for they were not, of course, allowed to whisper in class.

The pupils had been sitting quietly a minute or two when an electric bell in the room rang. This was the signal for the children to march to the big assembly hall where the morning exercises were held.

"Attention!" called Miss Skell, who taught Bert and Nan. "Rise! Turn! March!"

There was the tramping of a hundred feet and the children were on their way to the auditorium.

It was at the close of the exercises, after the Bible reading and the singing of patriotic songs, that the principal, Mr. James Tarton, stepped to the edge of the platform and said:

"Boys and girls, I have an unpleasant announcement to make. I am very sorry to have to speak of it. But an accident happened this morning. Perhaps some of you may know what it was."

By the gasps and murmurs that ran

through the room it was easy to tell that a number of the pupils knew about what the principal was going to speak.

"Some one—a boy I think it must have been, for I doubt if a girl could throw so hard and straight. Some boy broke the rule about snowballing within a block of the school," went on Mr. Tarton, "and threw a ball, or a chunk of ice, against one of the stained-glass windows of the church. The window was broken, and of course must be paid for. It is only right that the boy who broke it should pay for it. Now I am going to ask the boy who threw the snowball against the church window to be man enough to stand up and admit it. He will not be punished if he frankly confesses, but of course he or his father will have to pay for the broken glass."

Mr. Tarton stopped speaking and waited. It grew very still and quiet in the room. If any one had dropped a pin it could have been heard in the farthest corner. But no one dropped a pin. Nor did any one speak. Nor did any boy stand up to say he had broken the window.

The silence continued. The teachers, sitting in a row back of Mr. Tarton on the platform, looked at the faces of the boys and girls in front of them.

"Well," said the principal in a low voice "I am waiting."

Still no one got up. Some of the boys and girls began to shift uneasily in their seats and shuffled their feet. They were getting what an older person would call "nervous."

"It does not seem," went on Mr. Tarton, "that the boy who broke the window is going to be man enough to own up to it. I dislike to do this, but I must ask if any one here knows anything about it. I mean did any of you see any one throw a snowball at the church window?"

There was a further silence, but only for a few seconds. Then up went the hand of Sam Todd. Some of the girls gasped loudly, seeming to guess what was coming next.

"Well, Sammie," said Mr. Tarton kindly, "what do you know about breaking the church window? Did you do it?"

"No, sir!"

"Do you know who did?"

"Yes, sir!"

More gasps of surprise.

"Who broke the window?" asked the principal.

"Bert Bobbsey!" said Sam in a firm voice, and Nan was so excited that she cried out:

"Oh!"

Nor did the principal or any of the teachers scold her. But Bert was not one to sit quietly and be falsely accused. In an instant he was on his feet, raising his hand that he might get permission to speak.

"Well, Bert," said Mr. Tarton quietly.

"I didn't break that window!" cried the Bobbsey lad. "I didn't even throw a snowball toward it. I didn't do it at all!" His face was very red.

"Sammie, did you actually see Bert Bobbsey throw a snowball at the stained-glass window and break it?" asked Mr. Tarton, and his voice was stern.

"No, sir, I didn't really see him break the window," Sam replied. "But I saw a snowball in his hand. I saw him raise his hand to throw the snowball, and right after that I heard the glass crack. Bert Bobbsey did it!"

"I did not!" exclaimed Bert.

"Quiet! That will do!" the principal called, raising his hand for silence. "We will not go further into the matter here. Bert, come to my office after school, and you also, Sam. We will talk about the broken window then. The classes will now go to their own rooms."

The teacher at the piano began to play a lively march, but there was not much spring in the steps of Bert and Nan Bobbsey as they filed back to Miss Skell's room. Bert was hurt and indignant that Sam should accuse him of breaking the window. Nan, too, felt sure that her brother had not done it.

"Don't let him scare you, Bert!" whispered Charlie Mason, one of Bert's best chums, to the Bobbsey lad in the corridor. "We know you didn't do it."

Of course it was against the rule for Charlie to whisper thus in the hall, but he was not caught at it. Bert was glad his chum had spoken to him.

"Now, children," said Miss Skell, when her pupils were again in their seats, "we are going to forget all about the broken church window. Mr. Tarton will attend to that. And please forget that Bert has been mentioned as doing it.

"I, for one," and Miss Skell smiled down at the blushing Bobbsey boy, "don't believe Bert would do such a thing. I think Sammie must be mistaken. Now we shall go on with our lessons."

Neither Danny nor Sam were in the room with Bert and Nan, and for this the two Bobbseys were glad. Sam and his crony were in the same grade with Bert and Nan, but, because of its size, the class recited in two different rooms under separate teachers.

It took a little time for the class to quiet down after the unusual excitement, but at length the recitations were proceeded with.

It was when Bert and Nan were hurrying home at the noon recess with Flossie and Freddie that Nan said to her brother:

"Who broke that window, Bert? If you know you ought to tell, especially since they say you did it."

"Nobody says I did it except that sneak, Sam Todd, and he isn't telling the truth!" exclaimed her twin.

"Do you know who did it?" persisted Nan. Flossie and Freddie had run on a little way ahead to play with children from their own class, and did not hear what the two older Bobbseys were saying.

"I'm not sure," answered Bert, looking about to make certain no one was near enough to catch what he said, "I didn't actually see him throw the snowball, but I believe Danny Rugg broke that window."

"Oh, Bert, do you, really?" gasped Nan.

"I sure do! I can't prove it, for I didn't see him. But he had a snowball in his hand and he chucked it away when he was near the church. And right after that the window broke. But I'm not going to tell."

"Oh, Bert, maybe you ought to! Do you remember the time Mr. Ringley's shoe store window was broken?"

"Yes," answered Bert, "I remember that time."

"They said you did that," went on Nan. "But afterward old Mr. Roscoe said he saw Danny Rugg throw the chunk of ice that broke the window. And when Danny found out Mr. Roscoe had seen him, then Danny owned up that he did it. Don't you remember?"

"Yes, he broke Mr. Ringley's window," admitted Bert, speaking of something that happened in the first book of this series, "The Bobbsey Twins." In that volume you meet Danny Rugg as a bad boy, who was very unfriendly toward Nan and Bert. Then, after a fight, Danny seemed to have reformed, and he became a better boy.

"He's as bad as ever—breaking windows and things like that!" went on Nan.

"We don't know for sure that he did it," cautioned Bert.

"It would be just like him to do it!" declared Nan. "Are you going to tell mother?"

"Sure!"

And when Mrs. Bobbsey heard what had happened she advised Bert to speak nothing but the truth and not to accuse Danny unless he was sure that lad had broken the window.

"That's the trouble," sighed Bert. "I can't be sure, but I feel pretty certain that Danny did it."

"It will all come out right," his mother told him. "And of course you must not say that you broke the window if you didn't. Mr. Tarton is too fair a man to let you be accused without good proof."

And it was not very good proof that Sam Todd could give when later in the day he and Bert went to the principal's office. Sam told his story over again.

"Yes," Bert admitted, "I did have some snowballs in my hand. Danny Rugg and Sam had been throwing at John Marsh, and he ran to where I was. I was going to help John fight, but there wasn't any need. And I tossed away my snowballs before I got within a block of the school."

"So did I," said Sam. "And I think I

saw you throw yours at the church window, Bert. Maybe you didn't mean to break it, but you did."

"No, I didn't!" insisted Bert stoutly.

"I think we had better have Danny Rugg in here to see what he knows about it," suggested Mr. Tarton. "It would not be fair to punish Bert on just your say-so, Sammie. You might be honestly mistaken. Go out and see if you can find Danny and bring him in here."

But there was no need to go after Danny Rugg. Just as Sam was leaving the principal's office Danny came hurrying in, much excited.

"Oh, oh, Mr. Tarton!" he exclaimed.

"What is it?" asked the head of the school. And Bert found himself wondering whether Danny was going to confess having broken the stained-glass window of the church.

"Oh, Mr. Tarton!" gasped Danny. "I've lost my gold ring! My birthday ring is gone!" and he held up his hand. No longer did the gold band glitter on it.

CHAPTER IV

BAD NEWS

Mr. Tarton had not been principal of the Lakeport school a number of years without knowing how to deal with the boys and girls.

He was used to all kinds of excitement, having girls fall downstairs and stopping boys from fighting. And often the pupils lost things in school. So the news that Danny had lost his ring did not startle Mr. Tarton very much.

"Well, that's too bad, Danny," said the principal. "I'm sorry about your ring. I'll announce before the school to-morrow that you have lost it, and perhaps some one has found it. What kind of ring was it?"

"A birthday ring."

"Yes, I know. But was it gold or silver and did it have a stone in it?"

"It was gold, and all carved. It didn't have any stone in it, but on top it had the letters of my name—D. R. For Danny Rugg, you know."

"Yes, I know," returned the principal, while Bert looked at Danny and Sam rather soberly. For Bert did not like being accused of having broken the window when he had not even thrown at it, and he thought Danny should be man enough to own up that he did it.

"I was just going to send for you, Danny, to ask you about the broken church window," the principal went on. "But finish telling me about your ring, so I will know what to say when school starts to-morrow."

"Well, I had my ring on when I came to school this morning," Danny said. "And just now, when I was going home—I was waiting outside for Sam," he explained. "Just now I saw it wasn't on my finger. I went back in my classroom to look for it, but it wasn't there."

"Very likely you dropped it somewhere

around the school," said Mr. Tarton. "I will inquire about it. But now as to this broken window. Sam says he thinks Bert did it."

"But I didn't!" burst out Bert Bobbsey.

"Just a moment, please, Bert," said Mr. Tarton, in a low voice. "Did you see Bert break the window, Danny?"

"No, sir, I—now—I didn't exactly see him break it," answered Danny slowly. "But I saw him have a snowball in his hand."

"You had one yourself!" cried Bert. "And so did Sam!"

"I didn't throw it at the church, though!" Sam cried.

"Neither did I!" declared Bert.

Danny said nothing, but he did not look at Bert.

The principal questioned the boys for a long time, but he could learn nothing more. Sam stuck to it that Bert had broken the window, and though Danny did not actually say so, it was easy to see that he wanted Sam's story to be believed. And of course Bert said he did not break the stained glass.

"Well, Bert, do you know who broke the window?" asked Mr. Tarton, at last.

For a moment the Bobbsey boy was silent. Then in a low voice he said:

"Yes, sir, I think I know who did it. But I'm not going to tell."

Danny Rugg's face grew rather red at this, and he seemed very much interested in looking at something outside the window.

"Well," said Mr. Tarton, at length, "I can't make you tell, Bert, and I don't know that I want to. I hope that the boy who broke the window will be man enough to confess and pay for it. Meanwhile, we shall let the matter rest. You boys may go."

Danny and Sam hurried out ahead of Bert, who walked more slowly. Since morning many things had happened, and Bert no longer felt as friendly toward Danny as he had before.

"Danny's a whole lot meaner since he got so thick with Sam Todd," said Bert to himself, as he walked out of the school. He could hear the two cronies talking together just ahead of him.

"Did you really lose your gold birthday ring, Dan?" asked Sam.

"Sure I did!" was the answer. "Dad'll scold me, too, when he finds it out. I wish I could get it back."

"Don't you know where you lost it?" Sam wanted to know.

What Danny answered Bert could not hear, for by this time the two boys had run on ahead. They were making snowballs and throwing them.

"Trying to break more windows, I guess," murmured Bert, as he passed the church and looked up at the hole in the beautiful stained-glass window. Then he saw a man's head thrust out of the hole—for it was large enough for that, and Bert recognized the church sexton, Robert Shull. Mr. Shull was about to fasten a piece of plain glass over the hole in the colored window.

"Hello, Bert!" called Mr. Shull, for the Bobbseys attended this church and the sexton knew the twins.

"Hello!" Bert answered.

"I've got to mend this hole to keep out the

snow until this window can be fixed with new stained glass," the sexton said. "It's going to cost quite a lot of money, too."

"Yes, I guess so," agreed Bert.

"Some of you boys broke this," the sexton went on, his head still out of the hole. He was picking from the window frame small bits of broken glass that had not fallen when the snowball crashed through.

"Yes, I guess one of our fellows did it," admitted Bert.

"I heard it was you," went on Mr. Shull.

"Well, I didn't!" Bert cried.

"No, I don't believe you did. You aren't that kind of a boy. Maybe you know who did it?" Mr. Shull seemed to be asking a question.

"Yes, maybe I do," Bert admitted. But that was all he would say. He walked on toward home.

When Bert reached his corner and was about to turn down the street on which he lived, he saw Danny and Sam throwing snowballs at a signboard. The two cronies caught sight of him and Danny called:

"Want to get up a snowball fight, Bert Bobbsey?"

"No, I don't!" was the answer, not very pleasantly given.

"He's afraid of being licked!" taunted Sam.

"I am not!" cried Bert. "I'll snowball fight you any time I feel like it, Sam Todd, but I don't feel like it. And you needn't go around saying I broke that church window, for I didn't!"

"It looked just like you did it," Sam said, not quite so sure of himself as he had been.

"Aw, stop talking about it," advised Danny Rugg. "And say, Bert, if you find my gold ring I'll give you a reward."

"All right," answered Bert in a low voice, and passed on. He did not feel much like talking to Danny and Sam.

"I'll give you twenty-five cents!" Danny called after him. But Bert did not turn his head or answer.

On reaching home, Nan told her mother why Bert had been kept in. Mrs. Bobbsey felt sorry for her son, but she knew he had not broken the window, and she felt sure that in time the truth would be known.

So when Bert finally reached home, half an hour later than usual, he found his mother waiting for him. She asked him what had happened, and Bert told her.

"Do you really think Danny did it?" asked Mrs. Bobbsey.

"I'm almost sure of it," Bert answered. "If I could only prove it I'd be glad, for then everybody would know I didn't do it."

"Never mind," soothed his mother. "Perhaps, some day, you can find a way of making sure that Danny did it. Then your name will be cleared. But until you are sure, don't say that Danny broke the window."

"No, Mother, I won't," promised Bert.

"Did you say Danny lost his new birthday ring?" went on Mrs. Bobbsey.

"Yes and he was all excited about it."

"Well, of course it's too bad," said Bert's mother. "But he shouldn't have worn a valuable ring to school—especially at snowballing time. Things lost in the snow are hard to find."

Bert went out to play in the snow with his brother and sisters. He looked up at the evening sky and saw it covered with clouds.

"There's going to be more snow," Bert decided. "If a lot falls we can coast on the big hill, and we can make snow forts and snow men and everything!"

Bert, like the other Bobbsey twins, liked the fun that came with winter. He liked summer fun, also. In fact, Bert and the other three Bobbsey twins liked all kinds of fun, just as you and I do.

It was after the evening meal, when Mr. Bobbsey was telling Bert not to mind so much being accused of breaking the church window, that the doorbell rang. Dinah, the colored cook, big, fat and jolly, answered and came back with a yellow envelope in her hand.

"A telegram!" exclaimed Mrs. Bobbsey. "I hope it isn't any bad news!"

Every one grew quiet while Mr. Bobbsey opened the message.

"Well, it is bad news—of a sort," he said.

"What?" asked his wife.

"Uncle Rossiter is very ill," answered Mr. Bobbsey. "He wants you and me, Mary, to come to him at once. I think we'll have to go. It may be his last illness. We'd better start in the morning."

"Oh, will you take us with you?" begged Nan. "I remember Uncle Rossiter. Can't we go with you?"

"Take us! Take us!" begged Flossie and Freddie.

Mr. Bobbsey shook his head.

"No," he answered slowly, "it would be out of the question to take you twins. You'll have to stay at home and keep house by yourselves. Mother and I will need to leave in a hurry. We can't take you."

Sad looks were on the faces of all the Bobbsey twins.

CHAPTER V

MR. BOBBSEY got out some railroad time-tables and began looking at them, trying to decide how early he and his wife must leave the next day to get to Uncle Rossiter's home, which was several hundred miles away.

"Is Uncle Rossiter very sick?" asked Bert of his mother, who was again reading the telegram that had arrived.

"I'm afraid he is," was the answer. "Poor old man! He is all alone in the world. Your father and I are the only relations he has left, so that's why he wants to see us."

"I do wish we could go with you," sighed Bert.

"You wouldn't want to quit school, would you?" asked his father, looking up from the time-tables.

"School isn't so nice when a lot of fellows

in it think you broke a window," grumbled Bert.

"Nonsense!" laughed Mr. Bobbsey. "You know you didn't do it. We know you didn't do it, and so do your friends. The others don't matter. And in time it will be found out who really smashed the glass."

"But if you and mother are going away and leave us here all alone, it won't be any fun," said Bert.

"Oh, I think it will!" cried Nan. "We can keep house by ourselves. I love to cook and wash the dishes."

"You won't be alone," Mrs. Bobbsey said. "Dinah will be here to cook and look after you. Sam will shovel the snow, if any more falls, and he'll look after the fires. You'll be all right with Sam and Dinah."

Sam Johnson was Dinah's husband, and though he was not as fat as was she, he was quite as good-natured and jolly.

"Besides," went on Mrs. Bobbsey, "I will ask a woman to come in to help you keep house, Nan."

"Who, Mother?"

"I'll send for Mrs. Pry."

"Oh, Aunt Sallie!" exclaimed Bert.

"Yes, Aunt Sallie," his mother answered. "She is a very good housekeeper and will look after you very well. She is a little deaf, it's true, but if you speak a little louder than usual and quite plainly, she will hear you. Flossie and Freddie aren't going to mind staying at home and keeping house while daddy and mother are gone, are you?" and she looked at the smaller twins.

"I like to keep house," said blue-eyed Flossie. "I'll help Nan wash the dishes."

"I like Aunt Sallie," said Freddie. "She makes nice cookies, and maybe she'll tell us stories."

"Oh, that'll be fun!" cried Flossie.

Mrs. Pry was an elderly lady who went about doing housework, and Mrs. Bobbsey had engaged her on other occasions when it was necessary for her to leave home for a time.

"I won't worry about the children when Aunt Sallie is with them," Mrs. Bobbsey said. "And now, if we are to leave early in the morning, Dick," she said to her husband, "we had better begin packing now. You do that and I'll telephone to the boarding house where Mrs. Pry lives and leave word for her to come early to-morrow."

Then began a busy time in the Bobbsey house.

"My, what a lot of things have happened since yesterday!" said Nan a little later when she was helping her mother put Flossie and Freddie to bed. "Freddie fell down a drain pipe, it snowed, the church window was broken, and now you're going away, Mother!"

"Yes, but daddy and I won't be gone any longer than we need be. my dear. And I know you will help Dinah and Aunt Sallie keep house."

"Oh, yes, I'll help—I love to!" answered Nan.

After the first shock of it was over and Bert and Nan had passed the disappointment of not being allowed to make the journey with their father and mother, the older Bobbsey twins rather began to like the idea of keeping house.

"I guess Aunt Sallie will give me all the cookies I want," thought Freddie, as he went to bed.

Mr. and Mrs. Bobbsey remained up later, to pack in readiness for the early morning start. Word came from Mrs. Pry that she would come as soon as she could.

"Now, doan you all worry, Miz Bobbsey," said Dinah to the children's mother when the taxicab came to take the travelers to the railroad station. "Sam an' me we'll look after de chilluns jes' same's if you all was heah!"

"I know you will, Dinah," said Mrs. Bobbsey. "Now, you be good children, won't you?" she asked, kissing them all again.

"We will," promised Nan.

"I'm going to make a snow man!" declared Freddie.

"An' I'm going to make a snow lady," said Flossie.

"I'll write you a letter," promised Bert, "and let you know everything is all right."

"Yes, Son, do that," begged his father. "And if it is found out who broke the window, put that in your letter."

Bert promised he would do this. More good-byes were said, Mrs. Bobbsey kissed the children for the third time all around, and then, trying not to let them see that her eyes were shining with unshed tears, she ran out to the taxicab, followed by her husband.

"Doan you worry now!" were Dinah's parting words. "Everyt'ing am gwine to be all right!"

But little did Dinah, nor any of the others, know what was going to happen when the Bobbsey twins began keeping house.

So early had breakfast been served that morning, in order that Mr. and Mrs. Bobbsey could take the train, that it was not yet time for school. So Bert went out to the garage where Sam Johnson was at work, for Bert wanted to fix something on his sled.

"I believe it's going to snow more," Bert said, looking up at the clouded sky, "and I want my clipper in shape for the big hill."

"Yes," agreed Sam, "I shouldn't wonder myse'f but whut we'd hab mo' snow. Feels mighty like it! Come in, Bert, an' shut de do'," he added, for Bert was standing in the garage with the door partly open as he scanned the sky.

"If it's going to storm," said the boy, as he got out his sled to mend one of the runners that was loose, "I hope it doesn't get too bad before dad and mother reach Uncle Rossiter's."

"Yes," agreed Sam. " 'Twouldn't be no fun to hab dem snowed in—fo' a fac' it wouldn't!"

Nan wanted to help Dinah wash the dishes, as she said she had time before school. But the fat, good-natured cook chuckled and said:

"Nebber mind, honey lamb. I got loads ob time. You jes' see dat mah odder two sweethearts am ready fo' school, bress dere hearts!" She meant Freddie and Flossie.

So Nan looked after the younger twins and then, as the hands of the clock pointed toward half past eight, the Bobbsey twins—all of them—went to their classes.

"But what about Aunt Sallie Pry?" asked Bert of Nan. "I thought she was coming to keep house for us."

"I guess she'll be at the house when we come home to lunch," Nan said.

That morning, before the assembled classes, Mr. Tarton mentioned Danny Rugg's lost birthday ring, speaking about the gold initials on top.

"If any of you children find Danny's ring," went on the school head, "either give it to him or bring it to my office."

Danny Rugg raised his hand for permission to speak.

"What is it, Danny?" asked the principal, while the whole school wondered what was coming next. Bert Bobbsey had a wild idea in his head.

"Maybe Danny's going to confess that he broke the window," said the Bobbsey boy to himself.

But what Danny said was:

"I'll give twenty-five cents to whoever finds my lost ring."

Some of the teachers laughed a little at

this, and even Mr. Tarton smiled, but he said:

"All right, Danny. You have heard the offer of the reward," he went on to the school. "And now about another matter. Yesterday it was said here that Bert Bobbsey broke the church window. I want to say that there is no proof of this. Bert says he did not do it, and we are bound to believe him.

"I do hope that whoever broke the stained glass will be manly enough to admit it, and pay for the damage to the church. I have heard from Mr. Shull, the sexton, that it will cost about ten dollars to repair the window."

Several of the children gasped at this. To most of them ten dollars was a great deal of money. And Bert thought Danny looked a trifle pale on hearing this news.

But nothing more was said about the broken window, and the classes marched to their several rooms and the school day went on.

Hurrying home at noon, the Bobbsey twins were rather surprised to find that Aunt Sallie Pry had not yet arrived to help Dinah take charge of the house.

"Maybe she isn't coming," suggested Bert.

"Oh, yes, she's suah to come!" Dinah stated. "Mrs. Pry, she done tellyfoam me dat she'd be ober dis ebenin'."

"Is anything the matter?" Nan wanted to know.

"She done say she got a li'l touch ob de misery in her back," Dinah explained.

"What's misery?" Freddie wanted to know.

"A sort o' pain," Dinah told him. "Now eat you lunch, honey lambs, so's you kin git to de head of de class when you goes back to school."

"I'm head of the class now, Dinah," said Freddie. "That is, I'm head of the boys. Flossie is head of the girls' side."

"Aw right, honey lamb!" chuckled Dinah. "Den you all had done bettah eat a good lunch so's you all kin stay at de head!"

Back to school went the Bobbsey twins, and when the classes were out later in the afternoon they hurried home again. As they reached the house a few flakes of snow began to fall.

"Oh, look!" cried Freddie. "More snow! Hurray!"

"Hurray!" cried Flossie. "Oh, won't we have fun!"

The wind began to blow and the snow fell more thickly.

"It's going to be quite a storm," said Bert.

"I wonder if mother and daddy won't be snowed in on the train?" said Nan. "Trains do get snowed up, don't they, Bert?"

"Sometimes they do, I guess," he answered. "But maybe mother and dad are at Uncle Rossiter's by this time."

"No, they won't get there until late to-night," Nan said. "It's a long journey."

"Oh, well, maybe they won't get snowed in," said Bert.

"I'm going to play with my sled!" cried Flossie. Then she opened her mouth wide, trying to catch snowflakes on her rosy tongue.

"So'm I!" added Freddie.

"Well, you may play out for a time," said Nan, acting the part of a "little mother." Then she told the two smaller twins to go in and get on their rubber boots and old coats, so if they fell down, as they often did when playing, no damage would be done.

After some jolly fun out of doors the Bobbsey twins entered the house by the side door to get ready for the evening meal. As they did so the bell at the front door rang.

"I guess that's Aunt Sallie," said Nan. "She telephoned that she'd be here about this time."

"Is the misery in her back better?" asked Freddie.

"I guess so," Nan answered as she went to the door, followed by the two smaller twins. And when Nan opened the door, there stood Aunt Sallie, her bag in her hand, and the snowflakes swirling around her.

"Well, my dears, here I am," she announced.

"We're glad you came," said Nan politely.

"How's your back?" asked Freddie.

"What's that?" cried the old lady. "You say the train ran off the track? Good gracious! I hope your folks weren't hurt! Oh, dear!"

"Oh, you're going to have boiled beets, are you? That's good! I'm very fond of boiled beets," and Mrs. Pry smiled and went on up-stairs, not knowing that she had misunder-stood Nan. But Nan did not take the trouble then to correct the old lady. She had all she could do, did Nan, to keep Flossie and Freddie from laughing out loud at Mrs. Pry's queer mistakes.

Bert and Nan at first felt a trifle lonesome because their father and mother had gone away, but this feeling wore off as the eve-ning advanced. There was a jolly little party at the table when the evening meal was served, and Mrs. Pry made many more queer mistakes because she did not catch just what the children or Dinah said. And as the Bobbsey twins were nearly always laughing, anyhow, a few laughs, more or less, at Mrs. Pry's mistakes did not matter. She did not know they were laughing at her, and, really, it did no harm.

"Anyhow, you can't help it," said Bert to Nan afterward. "I thought I'd burst right out snickering when I asked her to pass the bread and she thought I was saying I couldn't move my head!"

"Yes, that was funny," agreed Nan. "Is it still snowing, Bert?" she asked, as she got out her books, ready to do some studying for the next day.

"Yes, snowing hard," Bert reported as he held his hands to the sides of his face so he could peer out into the darkness. "Going to be a regular blizzard, I guess."

"Oh, Bert! I hope not that!"

"Why not?"

"Because, I don't want father and mother snowed-up."

"Oh, I guess a train can get through pretty big drifts before it's stuck. Don't worry."

Flossie and Freddie had gone to bed earlier, and about all they talked of was the fun they would have in the snow the next day.

"If it snows too hard they ought not to go to school," said Nan to Bert, speaking of the smaller twins.

"No, I guess it would be better for them to stay at home with Aunt Sallie and Dinah—if the snow's too deep," he agreed. "But maybe it won't be."

Flossie slept in Nan's room, while Freddie "bunked," as he called it, with Bert. Just how long she had been asleep Nan did not know, but she was awakened by hearing her sister calling her.

"Yes, dear, what is it?" asked Nan sleepily.

"I'd like a drink of water," Flossie answered.

"All right," Nan said kindly. She often got up in the night to get Flossie a drink. Now she slipped on her robe and slippers and went into the bathroom. "It's still snowing," said Nan to herself, as she listened to the wind blowing the flakes against the window. "I do hope mother and daddy will be all right."

Nan was carrying the water into her sister when the door of Aunt Sallie's room, farther down the hall, opened, and the old lady put out her head. Nan noticed the old-fashioned night-cap Mrs. Pry wore.

"Is anything the matter, Nan?" asked Mrs.

Pry. "Has anything happened? Are burglars trying to get in? If they are, telephone for the police at once. Don't try to fight burglars by yourself."

"It isn't burglars," answered Nan. "I was just getting Flossie a drink."

"What's that?" exclaimed the old lady. "You say Flossie has fallen into the sink? Poor child! But what is she doing at the sink this hour of the night?"

"Not sink—drink!" exclaimed Nan, trying not to laugh. "I am getting Flossie a drink."

"Oh—drink! Why didn't you say so at first, my dear? Well, I must get in bed or I'll have that misery in my back again."

Flossie turned over and went to sleep once more after taking the water. But Nan was a bit longer finding her way to dreamland. Somehow or other, she felt worried, just why she could not say.

"But I feel as if something were going to happen," she told herself.

However, Nan was a strong, healthy girl, and when you are that way you do not lie awake very long at night. So Nan soon dropped off to sleep and then the house remained quiet until morning.

"Oh, it snowed a lot!" cried Flossie, running to the window to look out.

"Get back into bed!" ordered Nan. "You'll catch cold in your bare feet. Is it still snowing, Flossie?"

"No, it isn't snowing but there's a lot on the ground."

"Well, I'm glad the storm is over," said Nan, as she got up to dress, after which she would look after Flossie.

So much snow had fallen in and around Lakeport that, though it was still early in the season, it looked as if winter had come to stay. Of course all the boys and girls liked this, though when Sam Johnson went out to shovel paths it can not be said that he liked the snow.

"Makes too much wuk!" Sam said to his wife.

"You ought to be glad you has yo' health, Sam!" chuckled fat Dinah. "An' when you comes in I's gwine to hab hot pancakes an' sausages an' maple syrup fo' you!"

"Yum! Yum!" murmured Sam. "Dat's good!"

"Are we going to have pancakes, too?" asked Freddie, overhearing this talk.

"Indeed you is, honey lamb!" said Dinah, smiling at him.

On the way to school, Danny Rugg and Sam Todd began throwing snowballs at Bert and John Marsh. Bert did not mind this much, since Danny and Sam were using soft balls. But pretty soon Joe Norton, a chum of Sam's, happened along, and he joined forces with Danny. This made three against two, and Bert and John were getting the worst of it when Charlie Mason, with whom Bert was very friendly, ran up.

"Let me get a shot at 'em!" cried Charlie, and he made snowballs so fast and threw them so straight, hitting Danny, Sam and Joe, that though the sides were even, Danny and his two chums turned and ran away.

"Ho! Ho!" taunted John. "You're afraid to stay and fight!"

"We are not," said Danny. "But it's almost time for the last bell."

"That's a good excuse!" laughed Charlie.

"I've got some horse-chestnuts in my pocket," said Sam to Danny as they ran on. "This afternoon we'll put some inside snow-balls and we'll soak Bert and his gang good and hard."

"All right," agreed Danny.

Though the snow had stopped falling, the skies had not cleared and the storm did not appear to be over, except for a little while. And there was so much snow on the ground that Mr. Tarton announced at the morning exercises that the children of the primary grades would be excused from returning in the afternoon.

"I also want to add," the principal went on, "that we shall do this winter as we have done in past years. If on any morning the weather is too bad, or the storm too heavy, to make it safe for you to come out, the bell will be rung three times, five strokes each time, as a signal that there is to be no school. Then you need not start.

"So, children, in case of a storm, listen about half past eight o'clock. And if the bell rings five times, then is silent, then rings five times more, then is silent, and then rings a last five strokes, that means there will be no school."

"I wish it would ring that way every day," whispered Danny Rugg to Sam, as they were marching back to their room.

"So do I," agreed Sam. "I hate school!"

And the worst of it was that his teacher heard him and Danny whispering, and each one had to remain in ten minutes later than the others that afternoon when school was dismissed.

Bert and Nan took Flossie and Freddie home at noon and left the smaller twins, who at once said they would go out and play in the yard which was covered with snow.

"Well, don't get your feet wet, my dears," cautioned Mrs. Pry. "The reason the principal let you stay at home was so you wouldn't get wet in the snow. And if you're going out in the yard to get wet feet, you might just as well go back to your classes."

"We'll be careful," promised Freddie.

"And if any snow gets down my rubber

boots, I'll take 'em off and empty the snow out," said Flossie.

It was Freddie who, a little later, thought of a way to have some fun. Floundering about in the snowy yard he saw back of the garage the big kennel in which Snap, the dog, used to sleep. A few weeks before this story opens, Snap had been taken sick, and had been sent to a dog-doctor to be cured. He was to remain away several months. So Sam had cleaned out the kennel and put it back of the garage.

"I know how we can have lots of fun, Flossie," said Freddie.

"How?" asked the little girl.

"We'll play we're snowed-in at Snap's kennel," went on the little boy. "We'll crawl inside and make believe we're at the north pole. It'll be nice and warm in the dog house, 'cause there's a blanket nailed over the door. It's like a curtain."

"All right—let's do it!" agreed Flossie. "And if we could have something to eat in the dog house it would be like a picnic."

"I'll get something to eat," offered Freddie.

"What'll you get?"

"Some of Aunt Sallie's molasses cookies. She just baked a lot of 'em!"

"All right—get some, and we'll play snowed-up in the dog house," said Flossie.

Mrs. Pry was glad to have Freddie ask for some of her cookies, since the old lady was rather proud of the way she made them.

"What are you going to do with them?" she asked, as she handed Freddie the cookies.

"Eat 'em," he answered.

"Of course, my dear, I know that!" laughed Aunt Sallie. "But where are you going to eat them?"

"Out by the garage." Freddie didn't want to say anything about the dog house, for fear Mrs. Pry or Dinah would say he and Flossie couldn't play in it.

"Dat's aw right," announced Dinah. "De honey lambs will be safe out by de garage, 'case as how my Sam's out dere. But don't stay out too late, Freddie."

"We won't," he promised.

With the cookies, he and Flossie crawled into Snap's kennel. It was plenty large enough for them, and they could almost stand up in the middle, though the sloping roof made it lower on each side.

As Flossie had said, there was a curtain, an old piece of carpet, tacked over the front to keep the cold wind out. And Sam had put some clean straw in the kennel, ready for the time when Snap should come back.

"Oh, this is a lovely place!" exclaimed Flossie, as she snuggled down in the straw.

"It's fun!" agreed her brother. "Now we'll pretend there's a big snow storm outside and it's all piled up against our house and we can't get out to find anything to eat."

"We don't have to," said Flossie. " 'Cause you got cookies, didn't you?"

"Yes," answered Freddie. "I got a lot of cookies."

"Then we'll make believe some is roast turkey and some is cranberry sauce, and it's 'most Christmas," went on Flossie. Soon the two children were pretending in this jolly way.

Bert and Nan were a bit late coming home from school that afternoon. Bert stayed in to do something for Mr. Tarton, and Nan helped Miss Skell clean off the blackboards.

But when the two older Bobbsey twins reached home they noticed that Flossie and Freddie were not in the house. It was getting dark, too—getting dark earlier than usual because of storm clouds in the sky.

"Where are Freddie and Flossie?" asked Nan of Mrs. Pry.

"Playing out in the garage," was the answer.

But when Nan went out there Sam was locking the garage for the night.

"Flossie an' Freddie?" repeated the colored man. "No, Nan, I haven't seen 'em. Dey haven't been out heah all dis afternoon!"

"Then where can they be?" faltered Nan. "Oh, I wonder if they can have wandered away and are lost! Oh, Sam!"

CHAPTER VII

SAM GOES AWAY

"Dose chilluns aren't lost!" declared Sam Johnson when he heard what Nan said.

"Are you sure?" asked the Bobbsey girl.

"Cou'se I is!" replied Sam. "Where could dey be losted at?"

"They might have gone away over the fields to roll a big snowball, or something like that," suggested Nan. "And then they might have wandered to the woods and now can't find their way back."

"No, I don't believe dat," said Sam. "You say dey came out to play in de garage?"

"That's what Mrs. Pry says," answered Nan. "Freddie came in to get some of her cookies, and when she asked him what he was going to do he said he and Flossie were going to play in the garage."

Sam shook his head.

"I been out here 'most all de afternoon," he said. "I didn't see Flossie or Freddie. Cou'se dey might hab slipped in when I went to de house to git a bucket of hot watah. I'll take a look around to make suah!"

He opened the garage again and turned on the electric lights, for it was so equipped. Then Nan and Sam looked all over the first floor without finding a sign of the children.

"What's the matter?" asked Bert, hurrying out to the garage, having heard from Mrs. Pry and Dinah that Nan had gone to bring in the smaller twins.

"Oh, Flossie and Freddie are lost!" half sobbed Nan.

"I don't zackly believe dey's lost," Sam stated. "Dey's jest in some place we don't know. I'll take a look upstairs. Maybe dey went up dere to play house."

"Oh, maybe!" eagerly exclaimed Nan. There was a sleeping room over the garage, but it was seldom used, Dinah and Sam having quarters in the Bobbsey house. But Flossie and Freddie had often gone to this bedroom to play.

However, they were not up there now, and Nan cried some real tears when several more minutes passed and her little brother and sister could not be found.

"Is anything the matter?" asked Mrs. Pry, who had thrown a shawl over her head and hurried outside.

"We can't find Flossie and Freddie," stated Bert.

"What's that? Is supper almost ready?" inquired the deaf old lady. "Why, yes, it will be in a minute. Bring the little ones in and we'll eat."

"We can't find them! We can't find Flossie and Freddie!" called out Bert, this time so loudly that Mrs. Pry heard.

"Oh, my goodness!" she exclaimed. "Why, they came in and got some cookies—at least, Freddie did. Have you called for them? Maybe they've fallen asleep in the snow. I've heard that being out in the snow makes one sleepy."

"Say, we haven't called!" said Bert. "I'll give a shout!"

He did. several of them. He called at the

top of his voice for Flossie and Freddie, standing outside the garage.

And then, to the surprise of all, Freddie's voice answered:

"Here we are! What's the matter?"

"Where are you?" asked Bert, for he could not locate the voice.

"In the dog house!" answered Freddie, and a moment later he and Flossie, rubbing their eyes—for they had fallen asleep—came around the corner of the building. Bits of straw were clinging to the children.

"Where in the world have you been?" cried Nan. "We've been looking all over for you!"

"We were in Snap's kennel," explained Freddie. "We went in there to play snowed-in."

"And we made believe the molasses cookies were turkey and cranberry sauce," went on Flossie. "And then we went to sleep."

"For the land sakes!" cried Mrs. Pry.

Sam Johnson was laughing. He picked up Flossie and Freddie in his strong arms and carried them to the house. Dinah was just getting ready to come out and see what the trouble was.

"Mah good land ob massy!" exclaimed the fat colored cook when she heard the story. "To t'ink ob mah honey lambs bein' out in de dog house!"

"It was a nice place, with clean straw," stated Freddie.

"An' the cookies were awful good!" added Flossie. "But we ate 'em all up and I'm hungry again."

"Suppah's ready," Dinah announced.

"And you mustn't go in the dog house again," said Mrs. Pry. "Next time we might not find you, or maybe you couldn't get out."

"Oh, we could get out easy enough," said Freddie.

Thus the lost ones were found, and though Nan laughed at how funny the two twins looked as they came, sleepy-eyed, out of the dog house with straw clinging to them, she had been anxious for a time.

That evening Flossie and Freddie went to bed early, for they were still sleepy from hav-

ing been out in the fresh air nearly all afternoon. Grace Lavine came over to see Nan,
and Charlie Mason called to play some games
with Bert.

"I came past Danny Rugg's house on the
way over," Charlie said to Bert. "What do
you think he was doing?"

"Breaking more church windows?" asked
Bert.

"Breaking church windows? What do
you mean? Do you think Danny smashed
the one near our school?" asked Charlie.

"Yes, I do," said Bert in a low voice. "But
don't say anything about it. I'm trying to
find a way to prove that he did it so I'll be
cleared."

"All right, I won't say anything," promised
Charlie. "But that isn't what I saw Danny
doing."

"Was he looking for his lost gold ring?"

"No, it was too dark for that. But he was
out in the lots near his house—he and Sam
and Joe and some other fellows—and they're
making a big snow fort."

"Getting ready to have a snowball fight, I

guess," suggested Bert. "Well, I'm not going to fight, if he asks me. I'd rather have a fight with some other crowd."

"So'd I," agreed Charlie. "And I know something else."

"What?"

"Well, I saw Sam Todd taking a lot of horse-chestnuts into the fort they're building. They're going to put 'em in snowballs to make 'em harder."

"It's just like Danny Rugg and his crowd!" growled Bert. "They never do anything fair! Well, none of our fellows will take sides against 'em."

"I guess not!" agreed Charlie.

Grace Lavine laughed when Nan told her about Flossie and Freddie having been "lost" in the dog house that afternoon.

"Oh, I think they're the cutest children!" exclaimed Grace. "Don't you just love them, Nan?"

"Yes, of course. But they're always into some mischief or other. I was glad mother wasn't here to be worried about them."

"When is she coming back?"

"I don't know—not until Uncle Rossiter is better, I guess."

"And are you twins keeping house all by yourselves?"

"Oh, no, we have Aunt Sallie Pry."

Just then Charlie, who was playing a game of checkers with Bert, made such a sudden "jump" with one of his kings that he kicked over a chair near him. It fell to the floor with a crash.

"What's that?" asked Aunt Sallie from the kitchen where she was helping Dinah with the last of the evening's work.

"It was only a falling chair," said Nan.

"Somebody combing their hair! Well, they made noise enough about it, I must say!" exclaimed the old lady, and Grace and Nan had to stuff their handkerchiefs in their mouths to keep from laughing aloud.

Charlie and Grace went home about nine o'clock, and soon after that the older Bobbsey twins went to bed. Nan was feeling lonesome and wished for her mother's return. However, she said nothing about it.

It was the next afternoon when Bert came

hurrying home from school that more news awaited him and Nan.

"Where's Sam?" Bert called to Dinah, as he hurried into the kitchen. "I want him to fix that runner on my sled. It came loose again. Where's Sam, Dinah?"

Nan gave a quick look at the colored cook and guessed at once that something had happened.

"Is anything wrong, Dinah?" asked Nan, for she noticed a sad look on the kindly black face.

"Yes, honey lamb, dey is somethin' wrong," Dinah answered.

"Is it Uncle Rossiter?" asked Bert. "Or is it——"

He was afraid to ask about his father and mother.

"No, honey, 'tisn't quite as bad as dat," said Dinah. "But Sam, he done had to go away."

"Sam had to go away!" gasped Nan.

"Is he sick?" inquired Bert.

"No, he isn't sick," Dinah answered. "But his brother down South is terrible sick, an' a tellygram come sayin' dat Sam mus' come right off quick. So he went on de noon train."

"Oh, well, maybe Sam's brother will get better," replied Bert.

" 'Tisn't dat I's worryin' so much about," explained Dinah. "But wif Sam gone dey isn't no man around de house now, an' we's likely to hab mo' bad storms. Dey isn't any man heah!"

"I can look after things!" cried Bert. "I can shovel snow 'most as good as Sam. And I can shovel coal, too."

"Oh, we'll be all right," added Nan. Though, deep in her heart, she had a feeling that keeping house with Sam, the big, strong protector gone, was not going to be as much fun as it had seemed at first.

CHAPTER VIII

BERT'S TUMBLE

TRUTH to tell, Dinah had worried more on the children's account than on her own when it was found necessary for Sam to go to his brother, after a telegram had been received calling him to the South.

"I kin git along by myse'f, without any man," Dinah had said to Mrs. Pry when they had talked it over before the children came home from school. "But wif Mr. and Mrs. Bobbsey away, I don't want mah honey lambs to git frightened."

"I don't believe they will," said the old lady. "The Bobbsey twins—especially the older ones—seem quite able to look after themselves, even if Sam has to go."

And so it proved. Bert took a manly stand nor did Nan seem much worried, or, if she was, she did not show it.

As for Flossie and Freddie, nothing worried them very much nor for very long at a time. In fact, they did not pay a great deal of attention to the going of Sam Johnson. They had seen him around in the morning, and he was gone when they came home. That was all there was to it. If Dinah had had to leave—well, that would be quite a different thing.

The short early winter afternoon was fading. It would soon be dark. Sam had brought in a lot of wood and had carried up a whole box full of coal before he went away, so Bert did not have this to do.

"But I'll go out and lock up the garage," he said to Nan. "Sam always does that the last thing at night, even if none of the cars have been taken out. Now I'll do it."

Mr. Bobbsey kept two automobiles, but neither was in use now that he and his wife had gone to Uncle Rossiter's.

"And be sure the house is locked up well, too, Bert," warned Mrs. Pry. "Go over every door and window to make sure. We don't want any burglars coming in, with Sam away."

"Huh! If any of dem burglar men come in, I'll fix 'em!" declared Dinah.

"What would you do?" asked Bert, looking at Nan.

"Hit 'em wif mah rollin' pin—dat's whut I'd do!' cried Dinah, shaking the rolling pin, with which at that moment she was flattening out the dough for a batch of biscuits.

"I guess that would fix 'em!" laughed Bert. "But I'll lock up everything so the burglars can't get in."

That evening when Flossie and Freddie had, as usual, gone to bed early and while Bert and Nan were studying their lessons, a knock sounded on the side door.

"My goodness! what's that?" cried Mrs. Pry, almost jumping out of the chair in which she was sitting mending stockings. Dinah was out in the kitchen, "setting" the pancakes for the next morning.

"Some one's at de side do'," said the colored cook. "I'll go see who 'tis."

"What's that?" cried deaf Mrs. Pry. "Did you say you fell on the floor, Dinah?"

"No'm, Miz Pry. I said I'd go to de do'!"

"I wonder who it is and why they didn't ring the front door bell?" asked Nan of Bert in a low voice. "Do you suppose it could be a tramp?"

"Supposing it is?" asked Bert. "I'm not afraid. Tramps won't hurt anybody."

"No. But he'd be awfully cold and want to come in," returned Nan.

But it was no tramp. The next-door neighbor, Mr. Flander, having seen Sam leave that day with a valise, guessed that the colored man had been called out of town. And knowing that Mr. and Mrs. Bobbsey had left, Mr. Flander called to see if the Bobbsey twins needed anything.

"Oh, thank you, we're all right," said Bert, when he learned who it was.

"That's good," Mr. Flander said. "No, I won't come in, Mrs. Pry. I just ran over the side garden instead of ringing the bell at the front door. Well, if you want anything just let me or my wife know. Don't let the

Bobbsey twins go hungry or cold, you know."

"I guess there's no danger of that," laughed Mrs. Pry.

The kind neighbor took his departure, and soon after that Nan and Bert went to bed.

One of the first things Bert did the next morning when he came downstairs to breakfast, was to put on his cap and run out on the porch.

"Where are you going?" asked Mrs. Pry, who let Dinah do the cooking while she managed the house and saw to it that the twins had plenty to eat.

"I'm just going out to look and see if it's going to snow any more," Bert answered.

"Land sakes! do you want more snow?" laughed the old lady.

"Sure we do," Bert answered. "There isn't quite enough for good sleigh-riding, and it takes a lot to make snow houses and snow forts."

When he came back into the house, Nan and the other children having in the meanwhile taken their places at the table, Bert shook his head.

"I don't believe it will snow to-day," he said. "We'll have to go to school."

"Of course you'll have to go to school," said Mrs. Pry. "You don't stay at home just because it snows, do you?"

"Well, if it was a bad storm we wouldn't have to go," explained Bert. "If it snows so hard in the morning that it's bad for going to school, we must stay home, Mr. Tarton said. The bell will ring five strokes, three times, and we stay home. But I guess it won't ring that way to-day."

"I guess it won't," agreed Nan. "But maybe the postman will bring us a letter from daddy and mother to-day."

"Oh, I hope he does!" exclaimed Bert. "It seems as if they'd been away a week, doesn't it, Nan?"

"Longer than that," Nan answered.

Just then Flossie began to tap her fork on her plate and exclaim:

"Make him stop! Make Freddie stop!"

"Make him stop what?" Bert wanted to know. "He isn't doing anything, Flossie."

"He was looking over at my plate," went

on the little girl. "Make him stop it! Now you quit, Freddie Bobbsey!"

"Looking at your plate! The idea!" laughed Nan. "As if that did any harm! What's the matter with you this morning, Flossie? Why don't you want Freddie to look at your plate?"

"'Cause he looks at it so hungry-like," Flossie explained. "He's eaten his own griddle cake all up, and the maple syrup, too, and maybe he's going to take mine."

"I am not!" cried Freddie.

"Well, you looked so!" insisted Flossie. "Now you stop looking at my plate!"

"Oh, don't be so fussy," said Nan. "Dinah will give Freddie another griddle cake, and you, also, Flossie, if you want one."

"I want one," Freddie quickly said. "I was looking at hers," he admitted; "but I wasn't going to take it."

Then Dinah came in with another plate of the smoking, brown cakes and peace was restored between the two small Bobbsey twins. A little later breakfast was over and the four children started for school

"If a letter comes from mother, please put it where we'll see it the first thing when we come in, Mrs. Pry," said Nan to the old lady.

"What's that? You've lost your ring?" exclaimed Aunt Sallie. "Oh, my dear, you must look for it. Lost your ring—that's too bad!"

"No, I didn't say anything about a ring!" answered Nan, speaking more loudly. "I said put mother's letter, if it comes, where we can see it the first thing."

"Oh, yes, my dear, I'll do that. I thought you spoke of a ring. I don't seem to hear so very well this morning. I think it must be going to snow again. My hearing is always worse just before a storm. But I hardly believe your folks would have had time to write yet. They'll be very busy with your sick uncle. But if a letter does come I'll take care of it."

"It's funny she thought I said ring," remarked Nan to Bert as they walked along to school. "And that reminds me—did Danny Rugg find his ring?"

"Not that I heard of," answered Bert. He

looked down at his bundle of books and suddenly exclaimed: "Oh, I forgot and left my arithmetic at home. I'll run back and get it. You go on with Flossie and Freddie."

"Don't be late!" cautioned Nan.

"No, I won't," promised her brother, as he sped back toward the house, only a few blocks away. Flossie and Freddie wanted to know where Bert was going, and Nan told them. Then she hastened on with them toward school.

But Bert did not find his book as quickly as he thought he would, not remembering where he had put it the night before, and when it was found, and he was hurrying back on his way to school, Nan and the others were out of sight.

However, Bert still had plenty of time, though he kept ᴗ a jog trot which soon brought him within sight of the school. But Nan and the others had taken a short cut, and were already inside the building.

Just as Bert was approaching the church, the stained-glass window of which had been broken by a snowball, the Bobbsey boy saw ahead of him Danny Rugg. Danny was alone, and before the trouble Bert would have run up and joined him, for he and Danny were friendly. But that was before the window was broken. Now Bert did not care to be friends with this boy, and so he hung back.

"I'll wait until he turns into the school yard before I go in," said Bert to himself.

But there was a surprise in store for him. Instead of keeping on to school, when he got in front of the church, a short distance from the school, Danny gave a quick look around. Just then Bert happened to be behind a tree. From here he could see Danny, but Danny could not see him.

And, as it happened just then, no other boys or girls were near the church. Seeing this, Danny Rugg gave a quick little run and darted inside the church, a side door of which was open.

"Well, what do you know about that!" exclaimed Bert, half aloud. "Why is Danny Rugg going into the church this time of morning? Maybe he's going to ring the bell for a joke."

But as he thought of this, Bert did not believe it could be done. The rope of the church bell was high in a belfry and the door was kept locked. Bert knew this because once some boys had gotten in and rung the bell in the middle of the night. Since then the bell rope room had been kept locked.

"But why did Danny go in the church?" asked Bert of himself again.

There was only one way which the question could be answered, and so Bert decided on doing a bold thing. He looked at the clock in the church steeple. It was barely half past eight, and he had plenty of time.

So, waiting until Danny should have had a chance to get well within the church, Bert followed, walking softly to make no noise. And all the while Bert was puzzling over the reason why Danny had entered.

Coming in from out-of-doors, with the ground covered with snow, which dazzled him, Bert could see hardly a thing in the dark church entry. The side door opened into a vestibule in the rear of the church.

Unable to see where he was going, Bert

stood still a moment. He knew that his eyes would become accustomed to the gloom in a little while, and he would be able to see better.

He listened, and heard Danny walking about.

"Why, he's going upstairs—to the balcony!" whispered Bert. "I can hear him going upstairs! I wonder why he's doing that?"

Bert took a few steps forward and then suddenly felt himself falling.

"Oh! Oh!" he gasped as he realized what had happened. He had stepped into an open trapdoor in the center of the vestibule floor, and was tumbling into the cellar of the church!

CHAPTER IX

NAN IS WORRIED

BERT BOBBSEY was not a long while falling through the trapdoor. In fact, it took hardly a second. But in that short time the boy had time to hear Danny Rugg come clattering down the stairs that led to the balcony of the church. And from the speed with which Danny ran, Bert guessed that the other boy was frightened.

"I guess the noise I made when I stumbled and yelled scared Danny," thought Bert. Later he learned that this was so.

But poor Bert did not have time to think of much. He felt himself falling, he heard Danny's frightened rush out of the church, and then Bert landed on what seemed to be a pile of old bags in the basement of the church.

Then Bert felt a sharp pain in his head, which struck something hard, and a moment

later stars seemed to be dancing in front of
his eyes—stars in the darkness. Then Bert
knew nothing more. He was unconscious,
just as if he had fainted.

And there the poor lad was, alone in the
dark basement.

Danny Rugg did not know who or what it
was that had made the noise. He did not
stop to inquire, but darted to the side door
of the church, and, making sure by looking
up and down the street that no one saw him,
he slipped out and ran on to school.

Nan Bobbsey, with the smaller Bobbsey
twins, had gone in some time before. Leaving Flossie and Freddie in their classroom,
Nan went to hers to do a little early studying.
She expected Bert to come in soon, and when
it got to be a quarter of nine and her brother
had not yet entered, though several other
pupils had, Nan was not worried. She
thought Bert, after going back after his arithmetic, had met some of his chums and was
having fun with them on the way to school.

Bert was seldom late, but often he and

some of his chums entered the classroom just as the last bell was ringing its last strokes.

But when the hands of the clock pointed to five minutes of nine, when Miss Skell was at her desk, and most of the other boys and girls were in their seats, Nan began to get uneasy. Each time footsteps sounded in the hall outside the room she hoped it would be Bert who was coming. But he did not enter.

The last bell began to ring. Nan moved uneasily in her seat. She did not want her brother to be late.

The last bell stopped ringing.

"Oh, dear!" thought Nan, with a sinking heart. For now Bert could not enter without being marked tardy. And to Nan, as well as to many other pupils, this was a sad thing to have happen.

Miss Skell took out her roll book and began to call the names of the pupils. They were arranged in alphabetical order, beginning with those whose last name started with the letter A. And of course Bobbsey, beginning with B, was soon reached.

"Bert Bobbsey!" called Miss Skell.

There was no answer. The teacher raised her eyes from the book and looked around the room.

"Bert Bobbsey!" she called again, for Bert was seldom absent and Nan could not remember when he had been late.

There was no answer, of course. For at that moment, though none in the room knew it, poor Bert was lying unconscious in the church basement.

Then Miss Skell looked at Nan, whose name was next on the list. She marked Nan as being present, and then asked:

"Is Bert sick to-day, Nan?"

"Oh, no, Miss Skell," said Nan, very seriously. "He started for school the same time I did. Then he didn't have his arithmetic and went back after it. I don't know what happened to him. I don't know why he isn't here."

Nan's voice began to tremble a little. A thought entered her mind that perhaps, when Bert went back to get his book, something had happened at home—either to Dinah or

Mrs. Pry—and Bert had had to stay to look after things.

"Or," thought Nan to herself, "maybe a telegram came with bad news about Uncle Rossiter—or mother or daddy—and Bert had to go out there."

But on second thoughts she hardly believed this possible. Bert would not start alone on a long journey without telling her.

Miss Skell saw that Nan was troubled, so the teacher said:

"Probably Bert had an errand to do that detained him. Or, after coming to school, Mr. Tarton may have met him downstairs and asked him to do something. I think that is it—Bert has gone on an errand for the principal. In that case I will not mark him tardy. I will wait until after the morning exercises."

Nan Bobbsey breathed a sigh of relief. After all, Bert might have been sent somewhere by the principal. The Bobbsey boy had often gone on errands for the head of the school, and this, of course, always excused one from being marked tardy.

Miss Skell went on calling the roll, and soon the boys and girls marched to the big assembly hall where the morning exercises were held. Mr. Tarton was in charge, as usual, and as Nan looked at the principal, up on the platform, she wished she could ask him whether or not he had sent Bert on an errand.

Miss Skell, however, seemed to know what was going on in Nan's mind, for when the class was back in its room the teacher said:

"Nan, you may go to Mr. Tarton's office to ask whether he sent Bert on an errand. Then come back and tell me."

The Bobbsey girl hurried down the stairs and into the office where Mr. Tarton sat at his desk. Many books were in cases about the room. The principal's office was rather a solemn place, and especially so for any of the boys or girls who were sent there when they had done something against the rules. However, Nan was easy in her mind on this point, though she was worried about her brother.

"Well, Nan, what is it?" asked Mr. Tarton. Though he had a large school, he knew nearly every pupil in it by his or her first name.

"Did Miss Skell send you with a note to me?" he went on.

"No, sir," answered Nan. "But she said I might come to ask about my brother Bert."

"What about Bert?" asked the principal, with a smile. "Has he been throwing any more snowballs? I won't ask if he has broken any more windows, for, even though Sam Todd says Bert did it, I have doubts in my mind on that point. But what about Bert?"

"Did you send him on an errand?"

"Why, no, Nan. What do you mean?"

"Bert isn't in his class. He didn't come to school. He started with me and ran back to get his arithmetic, and I—I don't know what has happened to him."

Nan's voice faltered and she was about to cry. Mr. Tarton noticed this and said kindly:

"Don't worry. We'll find Bert for you. Very likely when he got back home your mother sent him to the store. He may come a little late, but if he does, and has a good excuse, he will not be marked tardy."

"Oh, my mother couldn't send Bert to the store, because she and my father have gone away!" exclaimed Nan.

"Well, then some one at your house may have sent Bert to the store."

"Yes, Mrs. Pry or Dinah might," admitted Nan.

"We can soon find out," went on the principal. "You have a telephone, haven't you?"

"Yes, sir."

"I will call up and ask if Bert went anywhere. Wait a moment."

The principal was about to call up the Bobbsey house when he happened to think of something.

"Perhaps I had better not do this," he said to Nan. "It might be that Bert went off by himself. I don't mean that he played truant, Nan," he said, as he heard the girl gasp. "I mean he might have met some one from your father's office, or something like that. Those at your house—the servant or this old lady that you told me was helping you keep house—would know nothing about it, and it might worry them if we asked about Bert."

"I'll tell you what to do. I'll ask Miss Skell to excuse you, and you may go home to see if Bert is there. If he isn't, come back and let me know. Then I will do something else. You need not alarm Dinah or Mrs. Pry. I will ask you to go home to get me a certain book. Let me see, I remember Bert once brought to school a book of your father's containing a number of fine poems for recitation. I'll send you home to get that book. Then you won't worry the old lady. How will that do, Nan?"

"It will be a good plan, I think," Nan answered. "And I hope I'll find Bert there."

"Yes. Or at least learn whether or not he has been sent on an errand," added the principal. "Give this note to Miss Skell."

He hastily wrote one, and when Miss Skell read it she said to Nan:

"Get on your hat and coat and go."

The boys and girls in the room, noting that Bert was not present and seeing Nan go out, did not know what to think. It was very mysterious.

But it was more than mysterious to Nan

Bobbsey when she reached home and saw nothing of Bert. Mrs. Pry saw the girl coming up the steps and opened the door for her.

"Why, my dear, school isn't out already, is it?" asked the old lady.

"No, I came back to get a book for Mr. Tarton," Nan answered. "Did Bert get his arithmetic?" she inquired.

"Yes, he found it," said Mrs. Pry, "and he hurried right out with it. I told him to hurry so he wouldn't be late for school."

So Nan learned, without really asking, that Bert had not been sent on an errand by either Mrs. Pry or Dinah.

"Oh, where can he be?" thought poor Nan, as she hurried back to school with the book of poems. "What has happened to him? How can Mr. Tarton ever find him?"

CHAPTER X

A CALL FOR DINAH

How long Bert Bobbsey lay unconscious in the basement of the church he did not know. It seemed a very long time to him, but it was probably not more than an hour—perhaps not that long.

The last thing he remembered was seeing a lot of what appeared to be brightly dancing stars in front of his eyes. And he saw them even though it was very dark in the basement. This was caused when his head struck something. And Bert also remembered, as among the last things that sounded in his ears, the footsteps of Danny Rugg as he hurried out of the church.

And now, as Bert recovered consciousness, or "came to," as it is sometimes called, he heard some one moving about near him in the basement. He also saw a light glinting about.

At first the lad thought this was Danny Rugg, and Bert felt so ill and helpless that he would have been glad of help even from Danny.

"Hey! Hey!" Bert faintly called.

Then a voice answered—a voice which wasn't that of Danny—it was the voice of the church sexton, Mr. Shull. Bert remembered this voice very well.

"Good gracious!" exclaimed Mr. Shull. "What's that? Is any one here in the basement?" he asked.

Bert saw the light coming nearer and then he knew the sexton was moving about with one of those small electric flashlights.

"Is anybody here?" asked the sexton again.

"Yes, I am," answered Bert, but his voice was so weak that the man, as well as he knew Bert, did not recognize the tones.

"Who are you?" called Mr. Shull, coming nearer with the light.

"Bert Bobbsey," was the answer.

"Good gracious! how did you get here?

Why, you're hurt!" the man cried, as he flashed the light on Bert. "How did it happen?"

He saw Bert lying huddled on a pile of bags and old pieces of carpet just beneath the open trapdoor. But for the moment the sexton did not think of the opening in the floor above. So Bert said:

"I came in here——" He was going to tell why he entered, then he happened to think perhaps this would not be wise. He did not want to mention Danny Rugg. "I saw the door open and I came in," went on Bert. "It was dark, and I walked across the vestibule, and then I fell down the trapdoor. I guess I've been here a long while."

"You poor boy!" exclaimed Mr. Shull, laying his flashlight down on a box and leaving it still glowing as he raised Bert up. "I'm so sorry! I opened the trapdoor to throw down some old bags and pieces of carpet. Then I had to fix the furnace and I forgot about the trap being open.

"But you haven't been here so very long, Bert, for I only opened the church about two hours ago. It's only a little after ten o'clock now, maybe not quite that."

' Then I've been here about two hours," decided Bert, for he remembered it was about half past eight when he followed Danny into the church.

"Well, you don't seem to be hurt much," the sexton went on, as he saw that Bert could stand up. Mr. Shull flashed the light over the boy from head to foot. No bones were broken, though Bert's clothes were a bit dusty and covered with cobwebs. The boy put his hand to his head.

"Is that where it hurts you?" asked Mr. Shull.

"Yes, sir. I hit my head on something when I fell."

"It was this box," and the sexton focused his light on one that rested on the floor just below the opening of the trapdoor. "Let me see, Bert."

Very gently, while he held the light in one hand, so it was shining on Bert's head, the sexton passed his fingers over the lad's scalp.

"It isn't even cut," he said. "You're all

right. The blow made you unconscious for a time, but that's all. I'm very sorry it happened. I'll help you upstairs and get you a drink of water. That will make you feel better."

Bert did feel decidedly better after drinking some water, and then the sexton turned on an electric light in the vestibule and made Bert sit down in a chair.

"The first thing I'll do is to close that trapdoor," said Mr. Shull. "I don't want any one else falling down there."

Bert wondered how it was that Danny Rugg hadn't fallen down, but he decided the other boy must have passed to one side of the opening.

"There!" exclaimed Mr. Shull, as he slammed the trapdoor shut. "I shouldn't have left that open but I didn't expect anybody to come in the church at this time of day. And it's mighty lucky for you, Bert, that I had tossed those old bags and carpets down right under the trap. Falling on them probably saved you from having broken bones."

"Yes, I guess so," Bert said. He was glad the sexton did not think to ask him why he had come into the church. To tell that would mean to mention Danny Rugg. And, somehow or other, Bert wanted to keep this a secret. He had an idea that Danny had a secret reason for going into the church.

"And maybe I can find out why," thought Bert to himself.

He was feeling much better now, and when the sexton gave him another drink and then got a whisk broom and flicked the dust and cobwebs off Bert's clothes, the Bobbsey boy was almost himself again.

There was a lump on his head where it had struck against the edge of the box, and his head felt sore, while one of his shoulders ached. But Bert had been hurt worse than this playing football, and he was not going to mind now.

"Do you want me to take you home Bert?" asked the sexton.

"Oh, no! I have to go to school!" the boy exclaimed.

"I guess they'll excuse you from school

when they hear what's happened," said Mr. Shull. "But do you feel able to go back to your class?"

"Oh, yes, I think so," Bert said. His head was clearer now and did not ache so badly. "I'll be late, though, I suppose," he added.

"Just a little," chuckled the church sexton. "But I'll tell Principal Tarton about it, and he'll excuse you, I'm sure."

Making certain that Bert's clothes were now well brushed, Mr. Shull started for the side door of the church, keeping near the boy in case he felt "tottery on his pins," as the sexton spoke of it afterward, meaning that Bert might be weak in his legs. But he wasn't, and when he got out in the fresh, cold air he felt quite himself again.

Mr. Shull walked with Bert as far as the schoolyard gate, and there saw Henry Kling, the school janitor.

"Hello, Bert!" exclaimed Mr. Kling. "What's the matter? Your sister just came in. She's been back home looking for you."

"Nan has been looking for me!" cried Bert.

"Yes. You didn't come to school and she

was worried. Mr. Tarton let her go home, thinking maybe you'd been sent on an errand some place. But Nan just came back. She was 'most crying and I asked her what the matter was. So she told me. Where in the world have you been?"

"Down in the church basement," Bert answered, with a smile.

"Not playing hookey? Don't tell me you tried to play hookey!" cried the janitor, who liked Bert.

"No, I fell through a trapdoor," the boy said, and he briefly explained what had happened.

"Well, you'd better hurry right into Mr. Tarton's office and tell him about it," advised Mr. Kling. "The whole school will be looking for you if you don't."

You can imagine how glad Nan was to learn that Bert had been found.

She went back to tell Mr. Tarton that her brother had not gone on any home errand. Then, by telephoning to the lumber office, they learned that none of the men there knew any reason why Bert should not be at school

The principal did not know what to think. And then Bert came in, much to the surprise, but also to the joy, of his sister.

"Well, the lost boy is found!" exclaimed the principal. He smiled at Bert, for he could see that it was not the boy's fault that he was late for school.

Bert explained matters and again he was glad that no one asked him why he had gone into the church.

"I think you may be excused for the remainder of the morning, Bert," said the head of the school. "And you needn't come back this afternoon unless you feel quite well."

"Oh, I feel all right!" Bert was quick to say. "I'd rather stay now than go home. If I go home, Mrs. Pry will think I'm sick, and she might make me take some medicine."

"Oh, I see!" chuckled Mr. Tarton. "Well, suit yourself. Here is a note to Miss Skell, telling her not to mark you tardy," and he hastily wrote a few lines on a piece of paper.

"Thank you," said Bert.

Then he and Nan went to their room, where their entrance created no little excite-

ment. All the other boys and girls wondered why Nan had gone out and why Bert
came in late.

They found out at noon time, for Bert told
his story. But still he did not say anything
about having followed Danny Rugg into the
church.

Of course Danny heard the story of Bert's
tumble, and Danny must have known that it
was the sound of Bert's fall that had caused
the noise which frightened him away.

But Danny said nothing to Bert on the
subject, nor did Bert mention it to Danny.
In fact, he and Danny did not play together
any more. They were not exactly "bad
friends," but they were not on good terms,
and hardly did more than nod or say "hello!"
when meeting.

"I'm just as well satisfied," Bert said to
Nan when they were on their way home to
lunch that noon. "I don't like Danny any
more."

"Why did he go into the church, do you
think?" asked Nan, for of course Bert told
his twin about following the other lad inside.

I don't know why he went in," Bert answered. "It was queer. I wanted to find out. That's why I went in after him. But I didn't think there'd be a hole for me to fall into."

Nothing was said at home about Bert's fall, for he did not want Dinah or Mrs. Pry to worry needlessly. And he felt all right again, especially after a good lunch.

"Did any letter come from mother or daddy?" asked Nan.

"No, my dear," answered Mrs. Pry. "Perhaps one will come to-morrow. Don't worry —your folks are all right."

But that afternoon when it began to snow again, though Bert and the boys greeted the swirling flakes with shouts of joy, Nan felt much worried.

As the storm seemed likely to be a heavy one, as soon as she was out of school Nan hurried home with Flossie and Freddie. The younger twins had not heard the talk about Bert's fall, and so would not mention it to either Mrs. Pry or Dinah.

Bert did not go home with Nan and the

smaller children. He stayed to have some fun in the snow with Charlie Mason and John Marsh. And he had so much fun and felt so much better, after his fall, to be out in the air that it was not until it was almost dark that he ran home.

"Oh, Bert!" cried Nan, meeting him at the door. "Something has happened!"

"Uncle Rossiter!" cried Bert. "Is he——"

"No, it isn't about Uncle Rossiter," answered Nan. "Oh, I've been waiting and waiting for you to come home to tell you! Dinah has gone away!"

"Dinah gone away!" cried Bert blankly. "What for?"

It seemed as if the bottom had dropped out of everything with the faithful colored cook away from the house and with Sam also gone.

"What happened?" asked Bert.

CHAPTER XI

LUMBAGO

"Come on in and shut the door," said Nan before she took time to answer her brother's question about what had caused Dinah to go away. "Mrs. Pry doesn't like the cold. We must keep the house warm for her, she says."

"'Tisn't cold!" declared Bert, whose cheeks were rosy red from having been playing in the snow. But he hurried in, closed the door, and then, turning to Nan, while he listened to the voices of Freddie and Flossie having one of their endless disputes in the playroom, the lad asked: "What happened to Dinah? What made her go away?"

"It's on account of Sam," answered Nan.

"Do you mean Sam came back and took Dinah away?"

"Oh, no, Sam didn't come back," went on Nan. "That's the reason Dinah had to go —because Sam didn't come back."

"Say!" cried Bert with a little laugh, though he could see by the look on his sister's face that she did not feel very jolly, "this is like one of the puzzles Charlie Mason asks. Where in the world is Dinah, anyhow?"

"She had to go down South—I don't remember just where—to look after Sam," explained Nan. "Something has happened to him—he's sick, or something—and a telegram came for Dinah. She must have got it while we were at school, for when I got home, and I came ahead of you, I found Mrs. Pry all excited and Dinah was packed up, all ready to go. She wanted to wait until you got back, to tell you good-bye, but I told her to go, or else she'd miss her train."

"That's right," agreed Bert. "But how did she know Sam was sick? Who told her?"

"A telegram came, I told you."

"Oh, that's so—you did. So many things are happening that I forget about some of them. But did Dinah have to walk to the station and carry her bag? I wish I'd been here—I'd 'a' carried it for her."

"She didn't have to walk," explained Nan.

"Just before it was time for her to go Mr. Batten called up from the lumber office. Daddy left word before he and mother went to Uncle Rossiter's that Mr. Batten was to call up every day and find out if we were all right.

"So when Mr. Batten called, I told him about Dinah having to go down South where her husband, Sam, was sick, and Mr. Batten said he'd have one of the men stop around in an auto and take her to the station, and he did. So Dinah went down in style all right."

"I'm glad of that," Bert said. "But say, Nan, we're almost all alone, aren't we?"

"Yes, only Mrs. Pry left to keep house for us."

"Oh, I guess we could keep house all by ourselves if we had to," Bert said. "Don't you think so, Nan?"

"I guess so. But is your head all right now, Bert?"

"Oh, yes, it doesn't hurt at all."

"Why do you s'pose it was that Danny Rugg went into the church?"

"I don't know," answered Bert, as he

thought the matter over for a second or two. "Maybe he went in to see if he could mend the broken window so he wouldn't have to pay for it."

"How could he mend a broken window, Bert? It's got all different colored pieces of glass in it. Danny couldn't mend it, even if he could find all the bits of broken glass. They wouldn't stick together."

"No, I guess that's right. Well, I don't know why Danny went in. But if he goes again maybe I'll find out next time."

By this time the voices of Flossie and Freddie had become high and shrill. They were evidently having trouble of some kind. And as Bert and Nan stood talking in the hall, Mrs. Pry was heard to say:

"Freddie! Freddie! Stop that!"

Then Flossie's voice joined in with:

"Give me my doll, Freddie Bobbsey! Give me my doll else I'll tell mother on you."

"Mother isn't at home, so you can't tell her!" taunted Freddie.

"Well, I'll tell her when she does come home. Give me my doll!"

"I guess we'd better go see what it is," suggested Nan.

"Yes," agreed Bert. "Dinah could make Flossie and Freddie mind better than Mrs. Pry can. But Dinah isn't here, so we'll have to do it."

The two older Bobbsey twins hurried up to the playroom on the second floor. There they saw Mrs. Pry standing in the middle of the carpet, looking helplessly at Flossie and Freddie. The little girl was trying to pull one of her dolls away from her brother, who held on to it with all his might.

"Here, Freddie, you let go of Flossie's doll!" ordered Bert.

"Yes, make him give her to me!" begged Flossie.

"Shame on you, Freddie Bobbsey!" cried Nan. "Why do you want to tease your sister —and you're a big boy? Daddy used to call you his fireman, but he wouldn't call you that now!"

"Oh, well, I wasn't going to hurt her old doll," answered Freddie, as he slowly let go his hold on the doll's legs. Nan's appeal to him, and the mention of "fireman," which was his father's pet name for the little chap, made Freddie feel a bit ashamed of himself. "I wasn't going to hurt the doll," he said.

"Oh, he was too!" cried Flossie. "He was going to make her stand on her head."

"Well, that wouldn't hurt her," Freddie answered, with a laugh.

"It would so!" declared Flossie. "Once I stood on my head and it may me feel funny and my face got red and Dinah said the blood would come out of my ears if I didn't stand up straight, so I did. I don't want my doll to have blood come out of her ears."

"I don't believe that would happen," said Nan. "But Freddie should leave your doll alone and play with his own things. Now don't tease Flossie any more."

"All right, I won't," Freddie promised, for he was not a bad little fellow, only mischievous at times. And so was Flossie, for that matter. She wasn't a bit better than Freddie. Being twins, they were much alike in many things.

"I've been trying to keep peace between them, but I don't seem to know how to do it," sighed Mrs. Pry. "I hope now, with Dinah and Sam gone, as well as your father and mother, that you will be good children," she added.

"I think they will," said Nan.

"What's that? You're going to take them out on the hill?" cried the old lady. "Oh, I wouldn't do that! Don't take them coasting now. It's almost dark and supper is nearly ready."

"I didn't say I'd taken them to the hill," answered Nan. "I said they will be good children now."

"Oh, yes! Well, I'm sure I hope so," sighed Aunt Sallie Pry. "I must see the doctor about my ears," she went on. "I can't hear half as good as I could five years ago, or else people don't speak as plainly as they used to. Well, now that Bert is home, we'll have supper. Oh, dear, I hope we don't get any more snow."

"When's Dinah coming back?" asked Freddie, as he came out of the bathroom, where he washed his hands ready for the meal.

"Oh, pretty soon, I guess," answered Nan.

"When are mother and daddy coming back?" Flossie wanted to know.

"Well, I guess they'll come home pretty soon, too," said Bert, with a look at his sister. A little later, while Flossie and Freddie were taking their places at the table, Bert whispered to Nan: "Don't you think it's queer we haven't had a letter from mother since she went away?"

"Yes, it is queer," agreed Nan. "I wish we'd get some news. But maybe Uncle Rossiter is too sick for them to have time to write."

"Well, couldn't they send a telegram?" Bert inquired.

"Maybe they thought a telegram would scare us," suggested Nan. "Dinah was frightened when that one came about Sam."

"That's so," agreed her brother. "I guess maybe that's why mother didn't telegraph us."

"Or maybe the snow's so deep where they are that the mail can't get through," went on Nan. "Lots of times, in winter, they can't deliver the mail on account of snow."

"That's right," said Bert. "I guess maybe they're all right. Anyhow, there's no good of worrying. And we'll have fun keeping house by ourselves, won't we?"

"Lots of fun," agreed Nan.

However, a little later, it did not seem quite so much fun, for something happened that would not have happened, very likely, if Mrs. Bobbsey had been at home.

With Dinah away, it made more work for Mrs. Pry, who got the evening meal, though Nan and Bert helped all they could. They knew how to do many things about the kitchen and the dining room, for their mother had allowed them to help Dinah so they would have good training.

It happened that when Mrs. Pry was coming from the kitchen with a plate of slices of bread, Flossie saw her. All at once it entered into the mind of the little girl that she ought to help, as she had seen Nan doing.

So, climbing down out of her chair, Flossie, with the kindest heart in the world, ran to Mrs. Pry, calling:

"I'll help you, Aunt Sallie! Let me help! I'll carry the plate of bread for you."

"No, no, my dear!" objected the old lady. "You might spill the bread off the plate."

"Oh, no I won't!" cried Flossie.

"If she spills the bread, that wouldn't break," laughed Freddie.

"No, but she might drop the plate, and that would crack," Nan said. "Flossie, dear, go back to your place!"

But Flossie did not want to do this. She had made up her mind to help about the meal in some way. So she reached up to take the plate away from Mrs. Pry, and the old lady, naturally, held the plate out of Flossie's grasp.

"I'll jump up and get it!" the little girl cried. "Mother said I was to be good and help Dinah all I could. And now Dinah's gone, I'll help you, Aunt Sallie!"

"But I don't need to be helped, my dear,"

said Mrs. Pry. "I can carry this plate of bread."

"Oh, let me do it!" begged Flossie.

Her first jump was not quite high enough, so she leaped a second time, and, though Mrs. Pry held the plate above Flossie's head, the little girl got hold of it. She pulled it from the old lady's hands, but, instead of keeping hold of it herself, Flossie let it slip from her fingers.

Down fell the plate of bread to the floor. The slices tumbled off and the plate itself was broken in three pieces.

"Oh, now you've done it!" cried Freddie. "Oh, look what Flossie did! She broke a plate! Flossie broke a plate! Flossie broke a plate!" he cried in a sing-song voice.

Flossie looked at the damage she had done and then her lips began to quiver, her eyes filled with tears, and a moment later she burst out crying.

"Oh, don't tell mother!" she begged. "Don't tell mother! I didn't mean to break the plate! I wanted to help!"

"Don't cry, my dear," said Aunt Sallie kindly. "Of course you didn't mean to do it. It's all right. I guess it was only an old plate."

"The bread didn't bust, anyhow," observed Freddie. "I can pick that up and we can eat it!"

"Freddie Bobbsey, you stay right in your chair!" cried Nan. "Something else will happen if you get down. And, Flossie, never mind. You can help with something else. Go to your chair and we'll eat."

Bert picked up the pieces of plate while Nan gathered up the bread. Luckily the slices had fallen in the same sort of pile that Mrs. Pry had put them in on the plate, and only the bottom slice had to be laid aside because there might be dirt on it from the rug.

"I'll feed that to the birds to-morrow," said Bert, as he laid this slice aside.

Flossie stopped her crying and soon supper was going on merrily—that is, as merrily as was possible when the Bobbsey twins were without father, mother, Dinah and Sam.

Mrs. Pry did her best, and though she mis-understood a number of things that were said, on account of not hearing well, the children did not laugh at her. They felt sorry for the old lady.

Nan helped clear away the supper dishes, with Bert lending a hand now and then. Flossie and Freddie, forgetting all about their little dispute, played together until it was time for them to go to bed.

Bert and Nan did their studying for the next day, and then Bert went about locking the doors and windows, Mrs. Pry telling him to be especially careful.

"For burglars might come in, now that we're more alone than ever before," said the old lady.

"Do the burglars know we're alone?" asked Bert, grinning at his sister, for neither of them felt any fears.

"They might. You never can tell," an-swered Mrs. Pry. "Anyhow, don't leave any doors open."

And of course Bert would not do that.

Just before he and Nan went up to their

rooms, Bert went to the front door to look out.

"Is the weather doing anything?" Nan asked.

"It feels like snow," Bert answered. "It's cold and sharp out, and it's cloudy. Maybe it'll snow to-morrow. I hope it does."

"I don't," Nan said.

"Why not?" her brother wanted to know.

"Because if it does maybe we'll not get a letter from mother or daddy for a long time. Maybe they're snowed-up now and if it storms again they'll be snowed-up worse. I don't want any more."

"Well, maybe it'll come anyhow," Bert said with a laugh, as he closed and locked the door.

The children were soon sound asleep and were not disturbed during the night. Even Flossie did not wake up as usual and want Nan to get her a drink.

Nan awakened first the next morning. She looked at a little clock on her bureau and was surprised to note that it was half past eight.

"Oh, we'll be late for school!" she cried,

jumping out of bed. "Mrs. Pry must have forgotten to call us. Oh, dear!"

Nan hurried about, putting on her gown and slippers, to go and call Bert and also to arouse Freddie. Flossie had opened her eyes when she heard Nan moving. Then a voice from Mrs. Pry's room said:

"Nan! Nan, dear!"

"Yes, Aunt Sallie, what is it?" asked Nan. "Are you sick?" The old lady's voice sounded different, somehow.

"Yes, Nan, I'm afraid I'm sick," was the answer. "That's why I wasn't able to get down and cook the breakfast. The lumbago has hold of me in the back. The lumbago has gotten a bad hold of me. Oh, dear!"

While Nan stood in the middle of the floor, hardly knowing what to do, Flossie burst into tears.

CHAPTER XII

THE SCHOOL BELL

Poor Nan was upset by hearing that Mrs. Pry was ill in bed when the old lady should have been up getting breakfast, and Nan was also rather worried about not hearing from her father and mother, so that when Flossie burst out crying it seemed as though too many things were happening.

"Why, Flossie, what's the matter?" asked Nan of her little sister. Nothing special had happened, as far as Nan could see. Flossie had not fallen out of her bed, that was certain. "Are you sick, too, Flossie?" asked Nan.

"No-oo-oo, I'm not sick," sobbed Flossie. "But I—I'm afraid."

"Afraid of what?" Nan wanted to know. "There is nothing to be afraid of. It's morning. We're late, and maybe we'll be tardy

132

at school, but that isn't anything to cry about."

"I'm not—now—I'm not crying about school!" Flossie sobbed. "I'm scared about Aunt Sallie!"

In her bedroom across the hall the old lady heard.

"Don't be afraid about me, my dear," called Aunt Sallie. "I'm not as badly off as all that, though I don't believe I'm able to get around. The lumbago has me by the back."

"There! That's what I'm scared of!" cried Flossie. "I don't want the lumbago to get me! Shut the door, Nan!"

Then Nan understood, and so did Mrs. Pry.

"The little dear," sighed the old lady. "You won't catch the lumbago, Flossie. Little girls don't catch the lumbago."

"No, but maybe the lumbago will catch me!" and Flossie still sobbed. "Shut the door, Nan, and keep the lumbago out!"

Then Nan laughed and said:

"Why, I do believe she thinks the lumbago is a sort of animal! Do you, Flossie?"

"Ye-ye-yes," was the halting answer. "Isn't the lumbago like the wolf in Little Red Riding Hood?"

"Bless your heart, no!" chuckled Mrs. Pry, in as jolly a manner as she could, though it hurt her to laugh. "The lumbago is something like rheumatism. It catches one in the back and keeps them in bed. I've had it before. I'll be better in a few days. Bless you! the lumbago isn't a wolf, though it pains a lot. Don't be afraid. Though I don't know what you are going to do, Nan. I'm not able to get out of bed, I'm afraid."

"I'll manage all right," Nan said, though her heart was sinking with all the troubles that seemed flocking around. "I'll make you some coffee, as I do when mother has a headache."

"Do you think you can, my dear?" asked Aunt Sallie. "I'm so sorry I'm laid up with this lumbago!"

"I can manage," replied Nan bravely, while she hurried with her dressing. "We children will just have to keep house by ourselves in real earnest," she said to herself.

Nan was helping Flossie dress, and then she intended to hurry down to the kitchen to make coffee. Nan could get up a simple breakfast, her mother and Dinah having taught her this. But as Nan fastened Flossie's buttons she heard Bert moving around in his room.

"Whoop-ee!" yelled the boy as he danced around his apartment. "Oh, look, Freddie! It's snowing like anything! It's a regular blizzard!"

"Oh, let me see!" begged the small Bobbsey lad.

"Don't run around barefooted!" warned Nan from her room. "I don't want you catching cold, Freddie, for then I'll have some one else sick to nurse."

"Oh, is Flossie sick?" called Bert who, having looked from the window to see that it was snowing hard, had now begun to dress. "Is Flossie sick?" he called again.

"No. It's Mrs. Pry," Nan answered. "She has the lumbago in her back, and I'll have to stay home from school and nurse her. You and Flossie and Freddie can go, Bert—that is, if the storm isn't too bad. But you'll have to hurry. We're late!"

"Late! I should say we were late!" cried Bert as he looked at a clock on his bureau. "It's after half past eight and——"

Just then, above the noise of the swirling snowflakes hitting against the windows and the sound of the howling, cold wind, another noise came to the ears of the Bobbsey twins.

A bell rang out in the distance. Five strokes were sounded, then a pause and five strokes more. Another pause, then another five strokes.

"It's the storm signal on the school bell!" cried Bert. "The three fives! Hurray, no school to-day!"

He danced around the room, half dressed.

"Are you sure?" asked careful Nan.

"Sure!" answered Bert. "There it goes again!"

There was no doubt of it this time. Fifteen strokes rang out, five strokes at a time. It was the signal Mr. Tarton had told the children to listen for in case of a storm. And this surely was a storm! The wind blew harder and the swirling, white flakes came down more thickly.

"No school! No school!" sang Freddie as he began to dress.

"No school! No school!" echoed Flossie, as she followed Nan to the kitchen.

"Hush, my dears, not so much racket!" begged Nan in a low voice. "Mrs. Pry is sick, and she may not like noise."

"Oh, I'm not fussy that way," said the old lady who, in spite of her deafness, seemed to have heard what Nan said. "Don't keep the children quiet on my account. And you'll have to hurry, Nan, or they'll be late for school."

"There isn't any school," Nan said.

"What's that—some one fell over a stool?" cried Mrs. Pry. "Oh, dear! And me flat on my back with lumbago! Who fell over the stool, Nan?"

"Nobody," answered the Bobbsey girl. "I said there was no school!"

"Oh! No school! You mustn't mumble your words, my dear. I can hear every time if you speak out. No school, eh? I'm glad of that, for if there was, you'd be late and on account of me. Oh, dear, I wish I could be around to help with the work!"

"We'll do the work, Aunt Sallie," said Nan kindly. "Don't you worry or fuss. Just stay in bed and keep warm, and I'll bring you up some breakfast. Would you like a hot flatiron for your back?"

"Well, it would help the misery a lot," the old lady answered. "But I don't like to be such a bother."

"It isn't any bother at all," said Nan kindly. "Bert will help me get breakfast, won't you, Bert?"

"Sure," he answered, sliding down the banister rail. "But I've got to shovel the walks of snow."

"They can wait," said Nan. "There's no use shoveling walks until it stops snowing."

"I guess maybe that's right," agreed her brother. "Say, it's a big storm," he cried, as he saw how much snow had fallen in the night. "I hope father and mother are all right—and Sam and Dinah, too."

"Yes, so do I," agreed Nan. "And I hope some mail comes in to-day. I'd love to have a letter from mother."

Flossie and Freddie crowded eagerly to the windows to look out at the storm. The house was snug and warm, but outside it was cold and blowy, and though the small twins did not mind snow or cold weather they were just as glad, this morning, that they did not have to tramp out to school.

Nan had often watched her mother and Dinah get breakfast, and so had Bert, so together the two older Bobbsey twins soon had coffee boiling on the stove, and the oatmeal which had been made ready the night before was being warmed.

"I'm going to fry me some bacon!" declared Bert.

"Do you know how?" asked Nan.

"Sure I do," he declared. "Once Charlie Mason and I made a fire in the woods and fried bacon. It was good, too."

"Well, first I wish you'd get some oranges out of the pantry for Flossie and Freddie," said Nan. "Do that while I'm taking Mrs. Pry up this hot coffee," she added, as she filled a cup with the steaming drink and put some slices of bread and butter on a tray.

"All right—the oranges will be ready in a minute," laughed Bert. "First call for breakfast! First call for breakfast!" he shouted, as he had heard the waiters in the dining car announce as they came into the Pullman coaches on the railroad.

"It's fun being snowed-in like this, isn't it, Flossie?" asked Freddie, as he tried to see how flat he could make his nose by pressing it against the window.

"Lots of fun," agreed the little girl. "But I'm hungry. I want my breakfast, Nan."

"Bert will give you your oranges now," Nan answered. "And I'll dish out your oatmeal when I come down after I take Mrs. Pry her coffee."

This satisfied the smaller twins, and they laughed at the funny faces Bert made as he went about, pretending he was a Pullman waiter. In fact Freddie laughed so hard that some of his orange went down the

"wrong throat" and Bert had to pat his
small brother on the back to stop the
choking.

Nan carried the coffee into Aunt Sallie's
room. Mrs. Pry had not gotten out of bed
and the shades were drawn down over the
windows.

"Shall I make it lighter for you?" asked
Nan. "It's snowing again."

"What's that? You say the pig is out of
the pen? Land sakes, child, I didn't know
you kept a pig! Dear me, and Sam isn't here
to chase him back into the pen! Oh, the
misery in my back! If it wasn't for the lumbago I'd get after the pig!"

"I didn't say anything about a pig or a
pen," answered Nan, trying not to laugh.
"I said it was *snowing again!*"

"Oh, snowing again," Mrs. Pry remarked.
"Well, why didn't you say so at first, my
dear? Dear me! We're having a lot of snow
this winter, and early, too. That's right;
raise the curtains so I can see out. And
thank you for the coffee. Ah, it makes me
feel better," she said, as she sipped it.

"Is it all right and strong enough?" asked Nan.

"Plenty strong, and very good, my dear. You're quite a little housekeeper."

Nan thought that she would need to be, and so would Bert, if they were to be left alone with a sick woman to look after. But Nan said nothing about this.

She helped Mrs. Pry sit up in bed, for the old lady could hardly raise herself on account of the pain in her back. Nan propped the pillows up against her, and then started downstairs to get the hot flatiron, leaving Mrs. Pry sipping the coffee and eating the bread and butter.

As Nan started down she heard the shrill voices of Flossie and Freddie, and she heard Bert calling:

"Come back in here! Come right back in, you little tykes!"

"Oh, what are they doing now?" thought poor Nan.

CHAPTER XIII

SNOWED IN

NAN BOBBSEY was glad her brother Bert was at home, helping her keep house. Without Bert she felt that she never could look after things, see to Flossie and Freddie and nurse the sick Mrs. Pry. And when Nan heard her small brother and sister squealing this way, which always meant mischief of some sort or other, she was more than glad that she also heard Bert's voice calling to the small twins.

Nan got to the foot of the stairs in time to see Bert running out of a side door after Flossie and Freddie who, bare-headed and with no wraps on, had run out into the storm.

"Oh, you mustn't do that!" exclaimed Nan. "Bring them in, Bert!"

"That's what I'm trying to do," he answered, but he could not help laughing, so jolly and full of fun were Flossie and Freddie, though they were also full of mischief.

"Now, I have you!" cried Bert as he caught Flossie before she had time to get very far away from the bottom of the steps.

"But you haven't got me!" shouted Freddie, making a dash through the piles of snow on the ground and also through the cloud of swirling flakes falling from the sky. "You haven't got me!"

"But I will get you!" shouted Bert. "Here, Nan," he called to his older sister, "you hold this little tyke while I chase after this Freddie boy!"

Nan, with a sigh and yet with a little laugh, held Flossie, who, truth to tell, was herself laughing and giggling so hard at the trick she and Freddie had played on Bert that she could not have run much farther, no matter how much she wanted to.

Freddie had counted on Bert having to drag Flossie along with him on the second part of the chase. But when Bert turned Flossie over to Nan, that left him free to run, and he caught his small brother before the latter had taken more than half a dozen steps.

"Prisoner number two!" cried Bert, picking Freddie up in his arms and carrying him back to the house. "Lock 'em up, Nan!"

"I shall have to, if they aren't better," Nan said, with a shake of her head as she put Flossie down in the hall while Bert did the same with Freddie.

"No, you don't!" suddenly cried Bert, as he locked the door out of which the mischievous ones had darted. He saw Freddie making a sly attempt to open it again.

"What happened?" asked Nan. "I was coming down to get the flatiron for Aunt Sallie and I heard the children scream."

"They were only yelling for fun and because they played a trick on me," laughed Bert. "They wanted to go out and get some snow, but I wouldn't let them."

"Of course not!" agreed Nan. "The idea!"

"But we got out, anyhow, didn't we, Flossie?" laughed Freddie.

"Yes, we did!" she giggled.

"I went to the front door to see if the man had left the milk," explained Bert, "for he leaves it on the front steps when it storms too much to come around to the back. And when I opened the door these two prisoners," and laughingly he shook a finger at them, "wanted to go out and get some snow to bring in the house.

"I said they couldn't, and I only had time to get the door shut to keep them in. Then I went to the side door, leaving them trying to unlock the front door, which they couldn't do, because I took the key out," and with another laugh Bert held up the key. "But all of a sudden they crawled past me while I was looking on the side porch for the milk, and that's how they got out. I had to run after them."

"I was wondering what happened," said Nan. "Did you bring the milk in, Bert?"

"No, I didn't Nan. There isn't any milk."

"Oh, didn't the milkman come?"

"Guess he didn't," Bert answered. "It isn't the first time he's missed us in a storm."

"Well, I think we have enough left for to-day," said Nan. "I'm pretty sure there is a bottle in the pantry. But if he doesn't leave any to-morrow, Bert, you'll have to go after some. But I guess the storm will stop by then."

"I don't know," said Bert, while again he shook his finger at Flossie and Freddie who were laughing together in a corner, plotting more tricks, it is likely. "It looks as if it's going to snow for a week, Nan."

"Oh, I hope it doesn't do that!" she cried. "Mother and father would never get home and we'll never have any word from them."

"I guess there'd be some way out," answered Bert. "But I don't believe there'll be any mail delivered to-day. I could go down to the post-office after it, though."

"No, I don't want you to go out in the storm!" objected Nan. "I don't want to be left here all alone, with Mrs. Pry sick. Maybe you couldn't get back."

"I'll stay with you," promised her brother good-naturedly. "But is Aunt Sallie very sick?"

"Well, she has lots of pain in her back," explained Nan. "That's why I'm going to take her the hot flatiron. Then I must wash the dishes and see about getting lunch."

"Could we play picnic and make believe take our lunch to the woods to eat?" asked Flossie.

"Oh, that would be lots of fun!" cried Freddie. "We could make believe up in the attic was woods. Let's do that!"

"I'll see about it," answered Nan. "Now you look after them a little while, Bert, and I'll take this iron to Aunt Sallie. And don't you two little tykes dare to run out in the snow again!"

"We won't," promised Flossie.

Nan found the old lady moving restlessly about in bed with the pain of the lumbago in her back.

"Do you think I ought to get the doctor for you?" asked the girl.

"Oh, no, dearie, I'll be all right in a day or so," answered Mrs. Pry. "This hot iron will help a lot. Then if I had some of my liniment to rub on my back, I'd feel better."

"Shall I get Bert to go to the drug store after the liniment?" asked Nan.

"You won't need to do that, dearie," answered Mrs. Pry. "I have some of the stuff in a bottle in my valise. If you'll hand it to me I'll rub it on my back, and then I'll go to sleep awhile. I didn't sleep much all night. But I fell asleep toward morning, and I slept so hard I didn't wake up in time to call you to go to school."

"Well, there isn't any school, so that didn't matter," Nan said.

She found the bottle of queer-smelling liniment in the old lady's valise, and gave it to her. Then Nan said:

"Well, I'll go down now and wash the dishes."

"What's that?" exclaimed Mrs. Pry. "You say Bert is going out and try to catch some fishes? Land sakes, child! he never can catch any fishes in this snow storm! Don't let him go! Besides, I don't like fish, anyhow!"

"I didn't say anything about fishes!" replied Nan in louder tones. "I said I was going to wash the *dishes!*"

"Oh! Dishes!" murmured Mrs. Pry. "Well,

my hearing isn't what it once was. But I surely thought you said fishes."

Holding back her merriment, Nan went downstairs. Flossie and Freddie were so filled with joy over their plan of going up in the attic and playing they were on a picnic in the woods that they had become very good and quiet indeed, making no trouble for Bert, who had "picked up" the dishes, ready for washing.

"I'll dry them for you," he told Nan, and he added: "We might as well give Flossie and Freddie some crackers and cookies, and let them play up in the attic where they won't bother Aunt Sallie. They've got to do something to keep out of trouble, and they can't go out in the storm."

"Yes, we'll do that," decided Nan.

Accordingly, she put some odds and ends of cookies, cakes and crackers in two boxes and gave them to the smaller twins. Then Flossie got one of her dolls and Freddie took a little iron fire-engine, one of his favorite toys, and the small twins went up to the attic. Nan went up with them and remained a little while, to be sure it was warm enough for them.

"I'll keep up a good fire," Bert had promised, and he was as good as his word, for the attic was as "warm as toast." Bert knew how to put coal on the furnace, and though he could not toss on quite as big shovelfuls as could Sam, who always looked after the heater, Bert did very well.

With the small twins thus out of the way for a while and with Mrs. Pry feeling better because of the hot flatiron and the liniment, Nan and Bert had a chance to do some of the housework.

"How do you like keeping house, Nan?" asked Bert, as he dried the cups and saucers.

"Well, it's fun, but it's a little bit lonesome," she answered.

"I feel that way, too," Bert said. "If Dinah and Sam were here it wouldn't be so lonesome. But with them gone, and daddy and mother away, it isn't so nice. But we've got to stick it out, Nan."

"Of course we have," she said. "I wonder what I had better cook for lunch?"

"Bacon," quickly answered Bert.

"Ho! Ho!" laughed his sister. "You'd have bacon three times a day, I guess."

"Well, it's what fellows always have in camp, and this is like camp," Bert explained.

"It is, a little," agreed Nan. "My, how the snow keeps up!"

"And the wind, too!" added Bert as a sudden gust howled around the corner of the house, sending the hard snowflakes rattling against the windows.

With Bert to help her, Nan tidied the rooms and set the house to rights. Then she looked in the pantry and saw that they had enough food for another day. She caught sight of a package of prepared flour, out of which she had often seen Dinah make griddle cakes.

"We'll have griddle cakes and maple syrup for lunch," decided Nan.

"Hurray!" cried Bert. "That's better than bacon. But can you bake griddle cakes, Nan?"

"Of course," she answered.

"Let me turn them for you," begged Bert.

"I'll see," was all Nan would promise.

It was shortly before noon that Nan went to the side door to look out and see if, by any chance, the belated milkman had been along. But the door would not open, though Nan tugged at it. Then, looking from a side window, she saw that a big drift of snow had piled up on the steps against the door, to which, as well as to the door jambs, the snow had frozen.

"Oh, Bert, we're snowed-in!" cried Nan. "We're snowed-in, Bert!"

Bert came running from the kitchen at the sound of his sister's voice. At the same time, up in the attic sounded loud shouts from Flossie and Freddie.

"Oh, what else has happened?" wailed poor Nan.

CHAPTER XIV

NAN'S BISCUITS

BERT BOBBSEY at first thought something had happened to Nan when he heard her call out. But as he came in from the kitchen and saw her standing safely by the door, he asked:

"What's the matter with you?"

"Nothing is the matter with me," answered Nan. "But the door is snowed fast. We can't get out."

"We can go to another door then," said Bert, not much excited. "Once last winter we couldn't get the back door open because a lot of snow had drifted against it, and we had to use the front door. That's nothing."

"Well, maybe it isn't," Nan agreed. "But listen to that!"

She pointed upward, and Bert heard Flossie and Freddie in the attic screaming and shouting.

"Those tykes again!" Bert cried with a laugh as he started for the stairs. "I'll fix 'em!"

"Oh, Bert, you'll have to be kind to them!", pleaded Nan. "If you're cross and they start crying, they'll want daddy and mother and then we can't do a thing with them! And there's so much trouble now, with Aunt Sallie in bed. Oh, dear!"

"Don't worry," replied Bert. "I'll be kind to 'em, all right. I guess Freddie is just teasing Flossie. She always yells when he teases her. Don't worry, Nan. Everything will be all right."

"I hope so," sighed Nan.

"And I'll get a shovel and clear that snow away from the door when I see what's the matter with those two tykes," went on Bert, as he hastened upstairs. He liked to call his small brother and sister by the funny name of "tykes," which means a mischievous little person.

Hurrying up to the attic, Bert found the

cause of the trouble. Flossie and Freddie, tired of playing picnic in the "woods," had started a circus game, each one pretending to be an animal. When Bert got up there he saw Flossie lying on the floor with one foot and leg thrust through the lower part of a chair. Freddie was pulling his sister by the arms, and as her leg was caught between the chair rounds, she could not get loose. The chair was being dragged along with Flossie. She was crying and Freddie was shouting.

"What's the matter? What's the matter?" called Bert. "Stop this kind of play!"

"This isn't play," Freddie explained. "We were playing, but Flossie got her foot caught and she couldn't get it out and I can't pull it out!"

"And it hurts me!" sobbed Flossie. "Oh, Bert, have I got to stay here forever?"

"Of course not," answered Bert. "I'll soon have you loose. Stop pulling, Freddie. You'll only jam her foot in tighter. Let go!"

Freddie let go of Flossie's arms and then, as she lay on the floor, Bert turned her foot a little way around, so that it was crossways with the chair rounds, instead of up and down against them, and a moment later Flossie was free.

"Goodness!" laughed Bert, when he saw that his sister was not hurt, though she still sobbed, "it sounded like a den of wild animals up here!"

"I was a wild lion," explained Freddie.

"And I was an elephant," said Flossie. "Freddie said I must be a bad elephant and kick the old chair over. So I kicked and my foot went in and I couldn't get it out again."

"I pulled her and pulled her, but it didn't do any good," explained Freddie.

"I should say not—the way you were pulling!" laughed Bert. "But I guess you've had enough of playing up here. Come on downstairs. You must have frightened Aunt Sallie out of her wits, banging around the way you did and yelling."

"Could we see Aunt Sallie?" asked Flossie, as she and her brother followed Bert down the attic stairs.

"I guess so, if she isn't asleep," said Bert. "I'll look in her room."

When he did so he found the old lady sitting up in bed.   She smiled at Bert and said:

"Are there any birds up in the attic? Seems to me, Bert, I heard birds fluttering around up there."

The noise made by Flossie and Freddie had been very loud, so loud that Nan had heard it away downstairs.   But the deaf old lady had thought it was only the twittering of birds.   Bert wanted to laugh, but he did not He just said:

"No, there weren't any birds, Aunt Sallie. It was just Flossie and Freddie playing with a chair."

"Oh, you say Flossie cut Freddie's hair? She shouldn't do that!   She might cut him or herself with the scissors.   Besides, she is such a little girl she can't cut his hair straight.   Flossie shouldn't cut hair.   Moreover, I never knew that hair-cutting made so much noise."

"No, no!" explained Bert.   "Nobody was cutting *hair*.   I said Flossie and Freddie were playing with a *chair!*"

"Oh! Chair!" repeated Mrs. Pry. "You should speak a little more plainly, Bert, my dear. Don't mumble your words. But how are Flossie and Freddie, anyhow? I haven't seen them all day."

"They're out in the hall now," explained Bert. "They'd like to see you if you're not too sick."

"Bring them in, Bert. I'm feeling a little better now. Nan is a good nurse. The hot flatiron she brought me helped the lumbago in my back. Bring the children in."

Flossie and Freddie looked curiously at Aunt Sallie. They had never before seen her in bed, and as she sat up, propped against the pillows with a blanket around her and a cap on her head, Flossie exclaimed:

"Oh, you look just like the pictures of little Red Riding Hood's grandmother!"

"Do I, my dear?" asked the old lady. "Well, if I'm the grandmother, the lumbago in my back must be the wolf. Not a real wolf," she added. "Just make believe, you know."

"I know," said Freddie. "I was playing I was a lion up in the attic."

"And I was an elephant," explained Flossie. "And I got my foot caught in a chair and I couldn't get it out!"

"Well, you're all right now," said the old lady, with a smile. "Be good children now, for you'll have to help Nan and Bert keep house until I get better. It's a sad time."

"Oh, we like it," laughed Freddie. "We can stay at home and don't have to go to school."

"You say somebody lost his mule?" asked Mrs. Pry. "That's too bad! The mule was lost in the storm, I expect."

Flossie and Freddie looked at each other wonderingly, and then at Bert. They were not quite so used to the misunderstandings of the old lady as were Bert and Nan. So Bert, before his brother and sister should laugh at Mrs. Pry, made haste to say:

"They didn't say anything about a mule, Aunt Sallie. Freddie said he was glad there wasn't any school!"

"Oh, school! Yes! Well, there's no sense

in going to school when it's such a bad storm. But I guess it will soon stop!"

However, it did not soon stop. The small Bobbsey twins went downstairs from Mrs. Pry's room, and the snow was still falling and the wind was still blowing. Not that the little twins minded this—they liked it all the more, snug and warm as they were in the house.

But Nan, getting the lunch and putting another flatiron on to heat for Mrs. Pry's back, shook her head more than once as she looked out of the window.

"What's the matter?" asked Bert as he noticed how serious his twin sister seemed.

"I'm beginning to get worried about mother and daddy," answered Nan. "I don't see why we haven't had some word from them—a letter or a post card."

"I guess the mails are late on account of the storm," Bert remarked. "If we don't get any to-day, and I guess we won't, for I haven't heard the postman's whistle, to-morrow I'll go down to the post-office and ask if there are any letters for us."

"You can't go if it storms this way," Nan said.

"It will stop by to-morrow," declared Bert.

With her brother's help Nan managed to get up a nice little lunch for the family, consisting of some baked potatoes, an omelet, and some bread and preserves. She made toast for Mrs. Pry and took it up to her with a cup of hot tea. Flossie and Freddie begged to be allowed to help, so Nan let them carry the toast—each one had a slice wrapped in a napkin.

"They can't hurt the toast, even if they drop it," Nan whispered to Bert. But the small twins were very careful, and the toast arrived safely in the invalid's room.

"You are very good to me, Nan," sighed Aunt Sallie. "I think I will try and get around to-morrow."

"No, you must stay in bed until your lumbago is all gone," insisted Nan. "I'll bring you up another hot iron as soon as you take your toast and tea."

"Yes, heat is the best thing for lumbago," said Mrs. Pry. "That and my liniment will

cure me, I expect. But my liniment is nearly
gone. And how to get more I don't know."

"Bert will get it for you," offered Nan
kindly.

The afternoon passed. Bert got out on the
porch in his big coat and rubber boots and
cleared away some of the snow. Flossie and
Freddie wanted to go out with him, but Nan
would not allow this. She got the smaller
twins into a room where they could not see
Bert at work with the snow shovel, and told
them stories.

"How is it outside, Bert?" asked Nan when
her brother came in, having cleared the side
door against which the big drift had blown.

"Pretty bad," he answered. "It seems to
snow harder than ever, and the wind is blowing and it's getting colder. I'm glad we're
inside with a warm fire and plenty to eat."

"That's just the trouble," said Nan in a
low voice. "We haven't plenty to eat, Bert."

"Not enough to eat—what do you mean?"

"Well, I mean we haven't any bread. I
toasted the last of it for Mrs. Pry. There's
no bread for supper."

"I'll go to the store and get a loaf," Bert offered.

"No!" cried his sister quickly. "I don't want you to go out in the storm. You might get lost!"

"But what'll we do for supper?" asked Bert. "I've got to have bread and butter."

"We have plenty of butter," explained Nan. "I'll make a batch of biscuits," she added. "They're as good as bread."

"Better!" declared Bert. "But can you make biscuits, Nan?"

"I guess so. Mother's told me how and I've watched Dinah make them lots of times. You just mix up some flour, milk, baking powder, water and lard and roll it out and then cut the biscuits into round shapes and put them in a pan and bake them in the oven."

"It sounds easy," remarked Bert. "I'll help you."

When Flossie and Freddie heard what Nan was going to do, they, also, wanted to help.

"We can't all do it," laughed Nan. "But

you can come in the kitchen and watch me."

"Can I have some sugar on my bikset when it's baked?" asked Flossie.

"Ho! Ho!" laughed Freddie. "Listen to what she called 'em! Bikset! Bikset!"

"That's their name," insisted Flossie.

"'Tisn't!" cried Freddie. "It's buskit! Guess I know!"

"You're both wrong!" laughed Bert. "But no matter how you call them, they're going to be good when Nan bakes them. Now you two sit down in chairs where you'll be out of the way."

Nan told Bert what to bring her from the pantry so she could make the biscuits, and then, putting on an apron and rolling up her sleeves, she began.

As she had seen Dinah do, she mixed the flour and lard together first, kneading it with her hands.

"It's just like making mud pies," said Freddie.

"'Cept it isn't brown mud—it's white," said Flossie.

"I wish I could squeeze 'em like that," went on Freddie, as he saw Nan working up the dough.

"Well, you can't, so just you sit still!" Nan told him, with a laugh.

Remembering what her mother had told her, and what she had seen Dinah do, Nan soon had rolled the biscuit dough out on the floured board, and then with a shiny tin thing, she cut out little round, flattened bits of dough, which she put in a buttered pan, ready for the oven.

"I've got enough dough for two pans of biscuits," said the little cook. "So I'll set this first pan down in a chair and get another pan ready for the oven. Then they'll both bake at the same time."

"We'll have lots of buskits!" said Freddie. "I'm glad, because I like buskits!"

"And I'm going to have sugar on my bik-set, ain't I, Nan?" asked Flossie.

"We'll see," said the young cook, giving all her attention to cutting out the second batch.

Flossie and Freddie both liked to watch this part of the work, so they left their chairs to stand beside the table. They stood on their tiptoes, so eager were they.

"Now I'll put these in the pan, and pop them into the oven," said Nan, when the last of the biscuits had been cut out. "Sit down in your chairs, Flossie and Freddie, so you won't be in my way when I open the oven door."

Flossie and Freddie went back to where they had been sitting, and all would have been well if Flossie had taken the same chair out of which she had slid a little while before to watch Nan. But, instead, Flossie backed up to the wrong chair.

It was the chair on which Nan had set the first pan of biscuits, and a moment later Flossie "plopped" herself down right on top of the soft bits of dough!

"Oh! Oh!" yelled Freddie, but too late. "Look! Look! Flossie sat on the buskits! Flossie's sitting on the buskits!"

CHAPTER XV

BROKEN WIRES

Nan jumped so, because of Freddie's shouts and Flossie's screams, that she almost dropped the batch of biscuits she was just then putting into the oven. But she managed to get them in and close the door. Then she turned and said to Freddie:

"You shouldn't fool me that way! Oh, how you startled me!"

"He isn't fooling you," said Bert. "Flossie did really sit in the biscuits!"

By this time the little girl herself had come to know that something was wrong. She felt something soft in the chair where she had been sitting—something soft with a hard rim around it that had not been in it when she got up to watch Nan use the biscuit-cutter.

"Oh! Oh!" screamed Flossie. "What is it?"

"Don't yell so. You aren't hurt!" said Nan.

"But the buskits are hurt!" yelled Freddie. "They're all squashed flat! Look at 'em!"

This was quite true—Flossie had sat down rather hard on the biscuits and they were "squashed," as Freddie said.

"But you can roll 'em out again, Nan," suggested Bert. "They aren't spoiled. Flossie's dress is clean—I mean it was clean before she sat in the biscuits."

"Is my dress—now—is it dirty?" asked Flossie, trying to turn herself around to look at the back of her garment.

"It's all sticky dough and flour," stated Freddie. "You look like a buskit yourself, Flossie!"

"Oh, dear!" sighed the little girl, and she would have burst into tears but for Nan, who put her arms about her and kindly said:

"Never mind. Your dress will wash and the biscuits aren't hurt much. I can roll them out again, and I'll give you two with sugar on."

"Oh, all right," agreed Flossie, and her

face brightened. Then, as Freddie said, she "squeezed back" her tears, and they all laughed at the funny accident.

Bert picked most of the dough off Flossie's dress while Nan took the "squashed" biscuits from the pan, rolled the dough out again on the moulding board, and made that batch over. Soon they were baking in the oven with the others.

"They smell good!" declared Freddie, when his sister opened the oven door to see how the biscuits were browning.

"They'll taste a lot better," laughed Bert, while Nan took Flossie upstairs to put a clean dress on her."

In spite of the accident, Nan's biscuits turned out very well, only a few of them being burned, and the children ate many of them for supper.

"Has Dinah come back?" asked Mrs. Pry, when Nan took her up a tray with her supper on it.

"Dinah come back? No, what makes you ask that?" inquired Nan, in surprise.

"Well, I see you have hot biscuits," went

on Mrs. Pry, with twinkles in her eyes, "and I thought Dinah had come back to make them."

"No, I did it!" exclaimed Nan, and she felt very proud that Mrs. Pry should think the biscuits as good as those which Dinah could make.

"You made these biscuits! My, that's wonderful!" said Aunt Sallie, tasting one. "You are certainly a good little housekeeper."

This pleased Nan more than ever and the lonesome feeling that was coming over her again, as night began to fall, seemed to pass away for a time.

After supper, or dinner, as it was called when Mr. and Mrs. Bobbsey were at home, Bert and Nan washed and dried the dishes. Flossie begged so hard to be allowed to help that Nan let her dry a few.

"But you must be careful and not drop any, or they'll break," cautioned Nan.

"I'll be careful," promised Flossie.

But alas! She was wiping a saucer when Freddie, who was playing on the floor with his train of cars, made a sudden movement.

"Look out!" cried Flossie. "Don't jiggle me!"

But her small brother must have "jiggled" her, or done something, for the saucer slipped from Flossie's hands.

Crash! It fell to the floor, breaking into half a dozen pieces.

For a moment Flossie stood there, looking at it with open mouth. Then as she realized what had happened she burst into tears and gasped:

"Freddie made me do it! That's all your fault, Freddie Bobbsey. It's your fault!"

"Oh, it isn't!" cried Freddie. "I wasn't wiping the dish!"

"But you—you—now—you jiggled me!" sobbed Flossie.

"That's what he did," declared Bert, who had seen what had happened.

"Never mind, my dear!" soothed Nan. "It was an old saucer anyhow, and it was cracked."

"Was—was it?" faltered Flossie.

"Yes, it was," Nan replied, and this was

true. It was an old dish which had had a fall before. But this was the end of it. "Dinah often said she was going to throw that old saucer away," went on Nan. "Now I'll do it."

It made Flossie feel better to know that she had not broken a good dish. So she dried her tears. But Nan decided that she would take no more chances with letting the little girl dry dishes.

"You two go in the other room with Bert and pop corn," she suggested, looking straight at Bert to tell him to get the small twins out of the way. "I'll finish the dishes," Nan whispered to him.

"Oh, pop corn! Pop corn!" cried Freddie, dancing around. "How I love pop corn!"

"So do I!" echoed Flossie. "I'm going to have some pop corn, ain't I?" she asked.

"Sure!" said Bert.

A little later, when Nan had finished the dishes, she joined Bert and the small twins in the living room, where Bert popped corn over the gas log. Flossie and Freddie laughed as the kernels cracked with the heat, bursting out into queerly shaped, big, white objects.

"They look like crooked snowflakes," was Freddie's comment.

"But they taste better'n snowflakes," said Flossie.

Bert wanted to melt some sugar and pour over the corn, so he could make balls of it, but Nan said this would be too sticky. So they melted some butter, poured that into the pan of popped corn, and then sprinkled on some salt.

"Oh, you! It's good!" mumbled Bert as he filled his mouth with the crisp corn.

"Yes," agreed Nan, "it is. And it would be jolly fun here if only the storm would stop.

"It's snowing yet," remarked Bert as they grew quiet a moment and listened to the flakes striking against the windows.

Though the older Bobbsey twins were a bit worried over keeping house all by themselves, with Aunt Sallie Pry ill in bed, Flossie and Freddie were not at all alarmed. It was

a perpetual picnic for them, and they had so
much fun, playing about the room, eating
pop corn and playing they were sailors ship-
wrecked on a desert island, and rushing to
door or window to see the storm that Nan
had hard work to get them to go to bed.

But at last they were tucked in, and then
Nan came down to sit for a while with Bert,
having first gone in to see if Mrs. Pry needed
anything.

"We'll have to get her some more liniment
in the morning, Bert," Nan told her brother.

"Yes, I'll go to the store," he agreed. "I
don't mind the snow."

"Then you can bring in some bread," added
Nan.

"And I'll see if there is any mail for us at
the post-office," added her brother.

The Bobbsey twins were rather surprised
the next morning when they looked out and
found that the storm had stopped. At least,
the snow had ceased falling, though a mass of
gray clouds in the sky seemed to tell of more
to come.

"I can get out to the store now!" cried Bert

as he quickly dressed. "And I'll get the mail, too!"

"I'm coming with you!" shouted Freddie.

"So am I!" echoed Flossie.

"Not much, you aren't!" exclaimed Bert. "You'd freeze your ears off. It's cold out!"

He could tell this, even though he had not been out of doors, by listening to the "squeak" of the snow as wagons were drawn along the street in front of the house. For the snowfall had been so sudden that few sleighs were out as yet.

"Well, I don't want to freeze my ears," said Freddie.

"I don't, either," agreed Flossie. So they no longer teased to be allowed to go out and play.

Nan got breakfast and then gave Bert Mrs. Pry's liniment bottle to have filled at the drug store. She also told her brother what to bring from the store, besides bread. Then, well wrapped up and wearing his rubber boots, Bert started out. The snow was deep, and it was cold. as he had said. But he did not mind even though it took his breath to plow through it.

He stopped in the drug store first, and handed Mr. Renner the bottle to fill with liniment.

"How's everybody up at your house, Bert?" asked the druggist.

"We're all right—what there is of us," Bert answered. "My father and mother are away, and so are Sam and Dinah. And Mrs. Pry's in bed with lumbago. The liniment is for her."

"That's too bad," said Mr. Renner. "Winter isn't the best time to have lumbago—in fact, I don't know when it is a good time to have it. Quite a storm we had. Lot of trains stalled, wires down and all that, I hear."

"Trains stalled?" exclaimed Bert quickly. "When?"

"Oh, that happened yesterday when the storm was at its worst," the druggist said, and Bert felt easier, for he thought his mother and father had reached Uncle Rossiter's before they could have been snowed-in.

"And are the wires down?" Bert asked.

"Yes, a lot of telephone and telegraph wires are broken. My telephone is out of order and I don't know when they'll get it fixed."

Bert took the liniment and went on to the post-cffice. There he found a number of men gathered about the letter window. Mr. Anderson, the postmaster, was speaking to them and Bert listened.

"There isn't any mail in—hasn't been for a couple of days," said the postmaster. "I don't know when there will be any. A lot of mail trains are stuck in the drifts. And the wires are down to a lot of places so I can't get any word as to when the mail will arrive. You'll just have to wait—that's all. Blame it on the storm."

Bert felt a sinking feeling around his heart. Still he made up his mind he was going to ask if there was any letter from his father or mother.

CHAPTER XVI

A GREAT CRASH

WAITING until some of the men had moved aside from the delivery window, Bert made his way to it. Mr. Anderson knew the Bobbsey boy, for in the summer Bert had often gone to his father's lumber office, and, more than once, had been allowed to go down to the post-office for the mail.

"No letters for the lumber company to-day, Bert," the postmaster said, with a smile. "There were a couple yesterday, but Mr. Jones got them."

"I didn't come for the office mail, Mr. Anderson," explained the boy. "But the postman hasn't been at our house for two or three days. and I thought maybe there'd be some mail here for my sister or me."

"I'll look, but I don't believe there is any,

Bert," said Mr. Anderson. "None of the men went out yesterday, on account of the heavy storm."

He went back to the long table where the mail was sorted, but when he again approached the window there were no letters in his hands.

"Sorry, Bert, nothing for you folks," said Mr. Anderson. "You see everything is upset. The trains are late, and some are stuck in deep snow up further north, I hear. And the worst of it is that a lot of wires have been blown down so we can't get any word. Tell your mother the man will go out with mail as soon as any comes in."

"I can't tell my mother that," stated Bert.

"Why not? Is she sick?"

"No, but Mrs. Pry is. She came to keep house for us while mother and dad went away. Then she got sick, and Dinah and Sam went away, and——"

"You don't mean to tell me you Bobbsey twins are keeping house all by yourselves!" interrupted the postmaster in astonishment.

"That's what we're doing," answered Bert.

"That's why I wanted to get a letter—to hear if my father and mother were all right."

"Oh, I guess they're all right, Bert," said Mr. Anderson kindly when he had heard the story of the trip Mr. and Mrs. Bobbsey had to take. "It's only that the mails are late. Probably your folks have written you, but you won't get the letters for a few days yet."

"Nan and I wrote to them, telling about Sam and Dinah going away," explained Bert. "But I guess our letters didn't get to them, either."

"No," agreed the man at the letter window. "I don't believe they did. And you can't telegraph or telephone them, either, Bert, on account of the wires being down. But I guess things will be better in a few days."

"I hope so," murmured Bert, as he turned away from the window. Others were coming in to make inquiries. "Nan will feel sad about not getting a letter," thought the boy.

However, there was nothing he could do. So he left the post-office and went to the store to get the things Nan had said were needed— a loaf of bread, some condensed milk—since the milkman had left no bottles—and half a dozen other things.

Now that the snow had stopped, at least for a time, the streets of Lakeport were filling with people who had not been able to get out of their houses during the storm. Many others besides the Bobbsey twins needed to buy things to eat.

"Well, you've got quite a bundle to carry, Bert," remarked Mr. Fink, the grocer, as he did up the things the boy had bought. "Think you can manage it all?"

"Oh, yes," was the answer. "I've got to get the stuff home. Don't want to go hungry, you know. And it looks as if it was going to snow some more."

On his way home with the bundle of food, Bert saw Danny Rugg just ahead of him. Danny also had his arms filled with bundles, for he, too, had been to the store. Seeing Bert, Danny stopped and grinned.

"Plenty of snow for a snowball fight now," Danny said.

"I haven't any time to fight," answered

Bert, in no very friendly tones. He more than half suspected Danny had suggested to Sam the idea that Bert had broken the church window.

"Aren't mad, are you?" Danny wanted to know.

Bert was going to answer and say he was not exactly "mad" when Sam, coming along the street, called to Danny and the latter hastened off to join his crony.

"I'd just like to find out why you went into the church that time I fell down the trap-door," mused Bert, as he struggled along, for it was hard going. "It had something to do with the broken window, I'm sure."

The wind was rising again and it was very cold. The gale whipped snowflakes from the ground into Bert's face with stinging force.

"Maybe we'll have another blizzard," he thought. "It sure does look like more snow," and he glanced up at the gray clouds.

Bert reached home at last and found Nan trying to amuse Flossie and Freddie in the house. It was hard work, for the small twins, now that they could look out and see that the fall of snow had stopped, at least for a time, wanted to go outside and play in the drifts.

"I think it will be all right for them to come out with me for a little while," suggested Bert, when he saw how Flossie and Freddie were "pestering" Nan. "They can put on their boots, dress warmly, and I'll take care of them."

"Well, all right," agreed Nan. "But they mustn't stay out too long. Mother wouldn't let them if she were here." At the mention of her absent mother Nan felt her eyes filling with tears, so she quickly turned her head away.

"Hurray! Hurray! We can go out!" shouted Freddie, capering about the room like a pony in a pasture.

"And I'm going to make snowballs!" declared Flossie. "But don't you dare wash my face, Freddie Bobbsey!"

"All right, I won't," he promised, on his good behaviour for a time, lest Nan change her mind about letting him out.

"Did you get any letters from daddy or

mother?" asked Nan, as Bert put his bundles on the kitchen table.

"No mail, and the wires are down," he said. "But I guess we'll get a letter to-morrow."

"I hope so," sighed Nan. "Did you get Mrs. Pry's liniment?"

"Yes, here it is."

"I'm glad you got it," went on Nan. "She's asked for it two or three times. Her lumbago seems to be getting worse."

"Maybe we'll have to get the doctor for her," suggested Bert.

"Oh, I hope not," exclaimed Nan. "If she got very sick, I don't know how I could wait on her and look after the house."

"It would be hard," agreed Bert. "But maybe everything will be all right. Now I'll take Flossie and Freddie out for a while. It will make them sleep better to-night to have some fresh air."

He and the small twins had some jolly fun in the snow. Well wrapped up and with rubber boots which kept their feet and legs dry, Flossie and Freddie raced about, made snowballs and tossed them to and fro, and even began to make a snow man.

. But it was so cold that the snow did not pack well, or stick together. Snow must be a trifle wet to roll big balls or build snow forts and construct snow men to guard them.

However, Flossie and Freddie had lots of fun, and Bert was a good brother. He let them throw snowballs at him, though it must be said that Flossie and Freddie did not hit him often, for they could not throw very straight. And when they did hit Bert the balls did not hurt.

Then Bert pretended he was a horse and raced about with them through the drifts until the merry laughs of Flossie and Freddie could be heard by Nan who was taking Mrs. Pry up some more tea, toast, and preserves.

"Well, I'm glad they're having a good time," sighed Nan. "They'll be easier to manage after they've had some fun."

Poor Nan was not having much fun herself. But she was a brave girl, and she knew she and Bert must keep house until mother and daddy returned, or at least until Sam or Dinah got back.

No word had been received from either of the faithful colored servants since they had gone. But this would not have been surprising, even if the mail trains had been running since neither of them knew much about writing letters.

Panting and laughing, with rosy-red cheeks, Flossie and Freddie came into the house with Bert, stamping and brushing the snow off their feet on the side porch, from which Bert had shoveled most of the big drift.

"Oh, we had lots of fun!" panted Freddie.

"Lots of fun!" echoed Flossie.

"We're going out again after we eat," went on Freddie.

"I'll see about that," was all Nan would promise.

And after she had given the small twins something to eat and had gotten something for herself and Bert, the latter, going to the window, exclaimed:

"It's snowing again!"

And so it was.

"Oh, can't we go out?" cried Flossie.

"Just for a little while!" begged Freddie, for they seemed to know that with the white flakes again falling their outdoor fun would end.

"I'll take them out for just a little while," said Bert. "They'll be easier to manage when they get good and tired," he whispered to Nan.

So, once again, the small twins were bundled up, and Bert took them out in the snow. They played about for a time, but the storm grew worse quickly, the wind being cold and the snowflakes stinging the faces of Flossie and Freddie, so that soon they were glad to go in again.

Just as Bert had thought, letting Flossie and Freddie play out of doors made the small twins sleepy, and they were ready for bed much earlier than usual that evening.

Bert and Nan were also tired, so about ten o'clock the Bobbsey house was quiet and dark, every one being in bed. The last thing Bert remembered hearing was the howl of the wind outside and the tinkle of snowflakes against the windows.

"It's storming hard again," he said to himself.

And the first thing he heard, when he awakened in the dim, gray light of morning, was still the noise of the storm.

"It kept up all night," thought Bert. "My, but the snow will be deep! And how that wind blows! It shakes the house!"

He was aware of a furious blast howling outside. And really, at times, the house trembled.

"Oh, Bert!" called Nan from her room. "Are you awake?"

"Yes, I'm going to get right up."

"Oh, it's a terrible storm, isn't it?"

"Yes, I guess it's pretty bad," admitted her brother. "But we'll be all right."

Hardly had he spoken than the wind howled louder than ever, and to the ears of the Bobbsey twins came the sound of a great crash. It was the noise of breaking wood and shattered glass.

"What's that?" cried Nan.

CHAPTER XVII

BERT FALLS OFF

BERT BOBBSEY did not know what had caused that crashing sound any more than did Nan. For a few moments he was frightened, as was his sister. Certainly that crash was enough to scare any one, coming as it did in the midst of the storm. And when you take four children, none of them very old, and put them in a house all alone, except for Aunt Sallie Pry, ill in bed, there is some reason for them to be afraid.

"Oh, what was it?" cried Nan again. "There it goes some more!" she went on, as the banging, crashing sound repeated itself. "What is it, Bert?"

"I don't know," he answered. "But I'll soon find out."

By this time Flossie and Freddie had been awakened. They, too, heard the terrifying noise and the banging which jarred the house.

"Maybe that's Santa Claus coming down the chimney," suggested Flossie.

"It's too early for Santa Claus," called Freddie as he quickly began to dress. "But maybe it's an airship, Bert, and it banged into our chimney. It sounds like a chimney, doesn't it?"

"It sounds like almost anything," Bert answered as he made haste in putting on his clothes.

In her room Aunt Sallie had caught the word "chimney," spoken by Flossie and Freddie, but she had not heard what else the small twins said. She did hear the banging sound, however, and she called:

"Oh, Nan, what is it? Is the chimney on fire? If it is, throw a lot of salt in the stove. Salt will put out chimney fires," which was true enough, only the chimney was not blazing—at least, Bert and Nan hoped it was not.

Nan answered the old lady, saying:

"We don't know what it is, Aunt Sallie. I don't believe the chimney is on fire. Bert is going to look."

"Oh, Bert dropped a book, did he?" exclaimed Mrs. Pry. "Well, that's all right— you can't help dropping things once in a while, and you can't break a book by dropping it. But it must have been a very large book to make so much noise."

"Ho! Ho!" silently laughed Freddie as he was dressing with his brother. "She thought Nan said a book, but she said you were going to look."

"Don't laugh," whispered Bert. "Aunt Sallie can't help being deaf."

And as they did not want to agitate the old lady, neither Nan nor Bert told her that something worse had happened than the mere dropping of a book.

That some danger was at hand Nan and Bert were very sure. The crashing, banging sound kept up, and at times the whole house shivered and shook, and it was not the wind which was doing this, either.

"Bert, I am afraid!" whispered Nan, as she and her brother met in the hall outside their rooms. Flossie and Freddie had followed them.

"You needn't be afraid," Bert answered, quite bravely for a boy of his size. "I'll soon see what it is."

"Maybe somebody rolled a big snowball on our stoop," suggested Freddie.

"Or else a big icicle fell," added Flossie. "Is it snowing yet, Nan?"

"Yes, it's snowing hard, and the wind is blowing. But, Bert," she added, "I believe Flossie and Freddie are right—the noise is outside, it isn't in the house."

"It does sound outside," Bert said. "Let's listen a minute."

They stood quietly in the hall. Mrs. Pry, believing it was a book that had fallen which made the noise, was waiting patiently in bed until Nan should bring her a cup of coffee.

And as the twins listened there came to their ears that banging sound again, and this time it clearly came from the front of the house and not far from where they stood. Mrs. Pry heard the noise too, and she must have felt the house tremble.

"Is Bert dropping more books?" she called.

"I'll bring your coffee right away," Nan

answered, thinking this was the best thing to say, rather than to speak of their fears.

"Yes, my dear, I'll feel better after some coffee," said the old lady.

"The noise comes from there," and Nan pointed, as she whispered, to the big front "spare," or guest, room of the house.

"I'll go in and see what it is," offered Bert. "You shut Aunt Sallie's door so she won't get nervous."

It was well Nan did this, for as soon as Bert opened the door of the guest bedroom, out blew a blast of cold air, followed by a cloud of snow. In a glance Nan, Bert and the smaller twins saw what had happened.

A big branch from a tree in front of the house had broken off and had crashed through the front window of the bedroom, breaking out all the glass. Through this opening the cold wind was blowing the snow, until there was a pile of the white flakes on the floor. The limb was not broken entirely off the tree, but hung by a few shreds of wood. It was as though it was on a hinge, like a door, and each time the wind blew the branch swayed to and fro, banging against the side of the house and on the porch roof, which extended across the front of the house, and beneath the guest-room windows.

"That's what made the noise!" cried Freddie, pointing.

"And look at the snow on the floor!" exclaimed Flossie. "I'm going to make a snowball!"

"No you aren't!" cried Nan, catching her little sister by the arm as she was about to dash into the room. "Oh, Bert, what are we going to do?" Nan asked. "The window is all smashed."

"And maybe that branch will poke a hole in the side of the house," added Freddie, as the wind, swaying the limb, banged it up against the window frame. There was no more glass left to break.

"I'll soon fix this!" cried Bert. "I'll get a hatchet and chop the branch loose. Then it won't bang any more."

"But you can't put in a new window!" said Nan.

"We can tack a blanket or something over

it, and that will keep out the snow and wind," decided Bert. "I'll get a hatchet!"

It seemed to be the only thing to do. For, as Freddie had said, the branch, if left to sway to and fro, would keep hitting against the side of the house and might in time break the clapboards and smash a hole through the plaster.

"Can you chop that branch off?" asked Nan, anxiously.

"Sure!" declared her brother. "I'll just get out on the porch roof, and I'll soon cut through that limb. It only hangs by a few shreds. It'll be easy."

Nan saw what Bert meant to do. They went a little way into the guest room, but it was so cold, now that the window was smashed, and the wind blew the snow about with such swirling gusts that Nan thought the small twins might catch cold.

"Come out and we'll shut the door," she called, pulling Flossie and Freddie toward her. "That will keep the rest of the house from getting freezing cold until we can tack a blanket over the window."

"I'm going to help! Can't I, Bert?" asked Freddie.

"I'll see," was all Bert would promise. "You go ahead and make the coffee for Aunt Sallie, Nan, while I get the hatchet."

"And I want my breakfast!" cried Flossie.

"So do I," chimed in Freddie.

"Now, just go easy," advised Nan. "I can't do everything at once. Oh, dear," she sighed, "so many things are happening! I do wish mother and daddy would come back!"

"Oh, we'll get along all right," replied Bert. "This isn't anything. 'Tisn't half as bad as if the chimney had fallen down, for then we couldn't have any fire."

"No, I suppose not," agreed Nan. "But I'll be glad when you get that limb chopped off. Listen to it bang!"

As she spoke the wind suddenly whistled around the house in a burst of freezing air, howling and moaning, while the swaying tree branch banged louder than ever.

"Nan! Bert! I'm sure that was the chimney blowing down!" cried Aunt Sallie, for

Nan had opened her door when they came out of the cold guest chamber.

"No, it's only a tree branch near the house banging against the side," Nan answered.

"What's that you say? You're going to take the children for a ride? Oh, I wouldn't do that so early in the morning, Nan. It must be very cold," said Aunt Sallie.

"No, no! I said that noise was a tree branch banging against the side of the house," repeated Nan in louder tones.

"Oh, a tree branch," murmured the old lady. "I thought it was some one knocking at the door. Is my coffee ready, dearie?"

"I'll have it for you right away," was the answer.

So Nan made Aunt Sallie a hot drink while Bert went down in the cellar to get a sharp hatchet with which to cut loose the dangling tree branch. Nan managed to keep Flossie and Freddie quiet by letting them set the table for breakfast.

When she took up Aunt Sallie's coffee and toast, Bert followed up the stairs, having put on his rubber boots, mittens, and a warm jacket. For he would have to climb out on the snowy roof to cut the tree limb.

As soon as he opened the door out rushed more cold wind and snow. But he quickly closed it again, and Nan waited until he was inside before she opened Aunt Sallie's door, which she had gone up to close just before Bert was ready to begin.

On the carpet beneath the broken window was a pile of glass and snow. Nearly all the glass was broken out of the window, only a few jagged pieces remaining, and these Bert knocked out with his hatchet so they would not cut him as he crawled through.

The dangling branch was half way across the window, but there was room enough for Bert to dodge through without getting hit by the swaying limb. Once out on the sloping porch roof, covered as it was by a blanket of snow, the Bobbsey lad looked up to see the best place to start cutting.

As he had said, the branch was attached to the part that was not broken off by only a few shreds of wood. Chopping through these would cause the branch to fall, and it could then be pushed off the roof. But the place where he must do the cutting was above Bert's head.

"I've got to get something to stand on," he decided.

He looked around inside the room and saw a small box. In it Mrs. Bobbsey had packed away the lace curtains for the guest room. And when the curtains had been hung the box had not been taken out.

"I'll stand on that," Bert decided. He pulled the lace curtains of the window to one side. The curtains were wet with snow, but Bert thought he and Nan could take them down and dry them later in the day.

Bert first put the box out on the porch roof in the snow. Then he crawled out himself. As he did so the wind swayed the branch and it nearly hit him, but he managed to scramble out of the way.

Then, standing on the box, he began to chop at the shreds of the swaying branch. It was hard work, but the boy kept at it. The sharp hatchet shaved through the thin wood.

"One more shot, and down you'll come!" exclaimed Bert.

He aimed a hard blow at what was left of the shreds. The hatchet cut through them and the branch fell to the porch roof. No longer would it bang against the house.

But in making his last stroke, Bert reached over too far. He felt himself slipping. The box on which he stood slipped on the snow of the roof.

The next moment Bert toppled over, fell on his side, and went rolling toward the edge of the slanting roof.

"Here I go!" he cried, trying to hold himself back.

But there was nothing which he could grasp, and an instant later he slid over the edge of the roof.

CHAPTER XVIII

AUNT SALLIE IS WORSE

While Nan Bobbsey was putting breakfast on the table for Flossie and Freddie, and also for herself and Bert, the smaller twins were amusing themselves by running to and fro in the house. They ran into the front room, up to the windows, out of which they looked at the storm, and then they ran back into the dining room.

"Don't make so much noise!" begged Nan, while she wondered how Bert was getting along with cutting off the tree branch.

"We're playing horse," explained Freddie. "Horses have to make noise."

"He's the horse and I'm the driver," said Flossie.

"Come on!" cried her twin brother. "We have to go to a fire now!"

Into the front room the smaller twins raced again, and as they reached the windows they saw Bert fall off the roof. They knew it was their brother.

"Oh! Oh!" screamed Flossie. "Look at Bert!"

Freddie gazed for a moment. Then he rushed back to the dining room where Nan was putting the oatmeal on the table and cried:

"Bert jumped off the roof! Bert jumped off the roof into a snowdrift in the front yard! Oh, Nan, you ought to see him!"

Nan gazed wide-eyed at her small brother. Why should Bert jump off the roof, especially when he had a sharp hatchet? Perhaps something worse than this had happened.

Nan hurried into the front room, followed by Freddie. Flossie was still at the window looking out.

"Bert's stuck in a snowdrift," she reported. "Look, he can hardly get out!"

And this was true. So deep was the snow in front of the house, and so far down in the drift had Bert plunged when he toppled off the roof, that it was all the boy could do to scramble out. Still he was making headway, floundering about to reach the front steps.

Nan ran to the door and opened it.

"Bert Bobbsey!" she cried. "What did you want to jump off the roof for?"

"I didn't jump," Bert said, somewhat out of breath as at last he managed to free his legs and reach the porch.

"Freddie says you jumped," went on Nan.

"No I didn't! I fell," panted Bert. "I cut the tree branch—and—then I slipped—off the box. I was standing on a box. I rolled—off—the roof—but I'm not hurt because I—fell in a snow bank."

"Oh, I'm glad of that!" exclaimed Nan.

"You are?" cried Bert, with a laugh. "Well, you wouldn't be glad if you had as much snow down your back as I've got down mine!"

"Oh, I didn't mean that!" Nan exclaimed. "I mean I'm glad you didn't get hurt."

"So'm I," said Bert. "Falling in the snow drift, even off the porch roof, was like landing in a feather bed."

"The hatchet might have cut you," went on his sister.

"I dropped that up on the roof when I fell, I guess," stated Bert. "Well, anyhow, I cut the branch loose, and it won't bang any more. Now we've got to nail a blanket over the window so the wind and snow won't blow in."

"You better have your breakfast first," Nan suggested.

"No, I'm all snow now and I might as well finish," decided Bert. "But I guess you'll have to help me put the blanket on, Nan. I can't hold both sides up at once."

"I'll do that," his sister agreed.

"We'll help, too!" cried Freddie, speaking for himself and his twin sister.

"No, you two get your breakfast," decided Nan. "It's all on the table ready for you. And be good children, now."

"We will," promised Flossie. "I'll let Freddie eat out of my oatmeal dish if he wants to."

"Each of you has a dish," laughed Nan. "There's no need of sharing them. Now come on, Bert, and we'll fix that window."

Nan knew where her mother kept the extra bed clothes, and from the closet she took a heavy woolen blanket. Bert got some big tacks from his father's tool box down in the cellar, and then the two older Bobbsey twins began work to keep out the wintry blast which seemed to howl with glee as it rushed through the broken window.

Bert found where he had dropped the hatchet in the snow on the roof before he rolled off.

"I'll bring that in to hammer with, and we can stand on the box," he told Nan.

"Oh, what a lot of snow on the carpet! And broken glass, too!" exclaimed the girl. "Mother would feel badly if she saw this."

"I'll clean it up as soon as we get the blanket tacked on," said Bert.

It was not easy for him and Nan to put up the heavy blanket and tack it fast to the sides of the window. For the wind would blow hard every now and then, spreading the blanket out like a sail of a boat. But at last they managed to get it in place, and then the wind could no longer enter, nor did any more snow sift in.

"We'll have to get a glass man to fix the window," said Nan.

"Can't get anybody until after this storm is over," was Bert's opinion. "A glass man might fall off the roof and break the new pane he brought. I guess this will be all right for a while. Nobody sleeps in here, anyhow."

"Yes," agreed Nan, "it will be all right. It doesn't matter if this room is cold."

Bert got broom and dustpan and cleaned up the snow before it should melt on the carpet. He also picked up the broken pieces of glass, taking care not to cut his fingers, and put them in an ash can in the cellar.

"And now I guess it's time I had my breakfast," he decided, when everything had been made as nearly right as possible.

"I'll eat with you," said Nan.

"Haven't you had your breakfast, either?" asked Bert, in surprise.

"I haven't had time," explained Nan. "I

had to look after Aunt Sallie and the twins."

She and Bert were on their way to the dining room, when suddenly they heard the voices of Flossie and Freddie.

"Stop! Now you stop, Freddie Bobbsey! Quit, I'll tell Dinah on you!" Flossie wailed.

"Dinah isn't here!" retorted Freddie.

"Guess those two need more looking after," laughed Bert to Nan.

"Oh, they're always up to something!" she sighed, as she hurried into the dining room.

Nan and Bert saw Freddie trying to pull away from Flossie the oatmeal dish the little girl had been using. Flossie was clinging to one side of it, and at the same time shouting:

"Stop! Stop! Now you stop, Freddie Bobbsey!"

"Give me the dish! Let me have it!" insisted the little boy.

"Stop, Freddie!" called Nan. "Why are you trying to take away Flossie's dish?"

"She's through with it. She's eaten up all her oatmeal," Freddie said. "I'm going to take the dish out in the kitchen and wash it."

"No, you mustn't do that." said Nan.

"I want to help you wash the dishes!"

"Thank you, dear, but I don't need any help this morning," Nan said.

"And he sha'n't have my dish! I haven't eaten all my oatmeal!" wailed Flossie.

"Oh, you did so eat it all up! There isn't any left!" exclaimed Freddie.

"There is so!" retorted Flossie, trying hard to pull the dish away from her brother. "There's sugar and milk in my dish and I want it, Freddie Bobbsey."

Bert had a look in the dish over which there was such a dispute. There was only a very little milk on the bottom—hardly a spoonful. But sometimes Flossie could be very fussy over little things, and this was one of those occasions.

"Her dish is empty and it ought to be washed," Freddie said, and he would not let go his hold until Bert took his fingers off, saying:

"Come on, Freddie, I'll let you help me make the water wheel as soon as I've had something to eat. Let the girls do the dishes."

"Oh, all right," agreed the little boy. Then to Flossie he cried:

"Girls are cry babies and they have to wash dishes! Boys make things, and I'm going to make a water wheel!"

"I am not a cry baby, am I, Nan?" appealed Flossie.

"No, dear, you aren't, of course," Nan answered. "You mustn't call names, Freddie."

"Well, then why didn't she let me take her dish out when it was empty?" the little boy wanted to know.

"'Tisn't empty! I'm going to eat the rest of my oatmeal," said Flossie, and she began to scrape up with her spoon what little milk remained. There was hardly enough to show, but Flossie made as much work over it as though the dish were half full.

"You can help me with the dishes, Flossie, as soon as Bert and I have our breakfast," Nan said, and this pleased the little girl. And Freddie forgot about his dispute with Flossie when he thought of helping Bert with the water wheel.

The storm kept up all that morning, and

it was so severe that though Bert wanted to go to the post-office to inquire if any mail had come in, Nan would not let him.

"You might get stuck in a drift and never get back," she said.

"Pooh! I guess I could get out of a drift!" laughed Bert. "Didn't I get out of the one I fell into off the roof?"

But Nan was so worried over the storm and about being left alone that Bert said he would stay at home.

It was still snowing at noon when Nan served lunch. Though as she looked in the pantry she said to herself:

"Somebody will have to go to the store to-morrow or we'll not have much to eat. I don't believe the stores will deliver anything. But maybe Bert can get out in the morning if the snow stops."

After Nan had seen to it that things were put on the table for Bert, Flossie and Freddie, she carried something up to Aunt Sallie, without waiting to get anything for herself.

As Nan entered the old lady's room she saw Mrs. Pry tossing from side to side in the bed, just as Nan had once seen Flossie toss in a fever.

"Who—who is that?" murmured Mrs. Pry in a faint voice, as Nan set the tray of food down on a table near the bed. "Is that the doctor?"

"No. This is Nan Bobbsey," said the little girl. "Don't you know me, Aunt Sallie?" She feared the old lady was out of her head with fever.

"Oh, yes, I know you, Nan," was the low answer. "But I thought you were the doctor. When is the doctor coming?"

"Why, I don't know," and Nan was puzzled. "Did you want me to send for the doctor?"

"Yes, dearie, I wish you would. I called down to you to send for him, but I guess you didn't hear me."

"Flossie and Freddie were making so much noise, I guess I didn't hear you," said Nan. "But I'll get the doctor right away, if you think you want him."

"I'd better have him, Nan. I'm much worse, I fear. I'm very sick and the lumbago is worse. That liniment doesn't seem to help me any. Send for the doctor. Dr. Martin is the best one, and he doesn't live far from here."

"I'll have Bert telephone for him right away," promised Nan. "And see, I have brought you up something to eat."

"I'm too sick to eat, dearie," moaned Aunt Sallie. "Get the doctor as soon as you can."

Nan hurried downstairs and told Bert. He went to the telephone, but after waiting some time he heard no voice of the operator asking what number he wanted.

"I guess the telephone wires are broken, Nan," he said. "I'll have to go over to Dr. Martin's house to tell him to come."

"Oh, dear!" sighed Nan, and she looked out of the window at the storm which was still raging fiercely.

CHAPTER XIX

IN CHURCH AGAIN

There was no help for it. If the doctor was to come to Aunt Sallie to help her, Bert must go after him. The telephone would not work.

"It isn't far," Bert said to Nan when he had tried several more times to get an answer from the telephone operator. "I can soon push my way down to Dr. Martin's office."

"Maybe he won't come back with you," suggested Nan. "Maybe he'll think the storm is too bad for him to come out in."

"Doctors aren't that way," declared Bert. "They go out in any kind of a storm when anybody is sick."

So he made ready to go out, again putting on his boots and getting out his long overcoat and mittens.

In order to leave his legs free, when he wa

chopping at the tree branch Bert had put on a short "pea jacket," as sailors call them. But now to venture out on the streets in the storm, he decided his longer overcoat would be best.

Inside the warm, cosy house the storm had not seemed quite as terrible as it was to Bert when he stepped outside. At first the wind nearly took away his breath, and the snow-flakes, tossed this way and that way by the wintry blast, stung the boy's cheeks.

But he laughed and shouted, pretending that he was a soldier fighting the storm, and he floundered out into the drifts and down toward Dr. Martin's house. There were very few persons out in the tempest, which was, in fact, a blizzard. Bert saw no one whom he knew, but a man who was tramping his way through the snow called to the boy:

"Quite a storm!"

"That's right," panted Bert, stopping to get his breath.

"More wires down than before," the man went on. "And a lot of trains are stuck in the snow."

Bert felt a sinking feeling in his heart, and he hoped his father and mother had not started back from Uncle Rossiter's only to be snowed-in. Bert decided he would say nothing to Nan about what this man had told him.

Floundering on through the snow, falling down once, but getting up quickly again with a laugh, Bert at last reached the doctor's house and rang the bell. A maid let him in the office.

"The doctor will see you in a few minutes," she said.

"I don't want him to see me," replied Bert. "I'm not sick. It's Aunt Sallie Pry. She's staying at our house and she has the lumbago."

The maid smiled at the boy, and the doctor, who happened to be in the next room, opened the door, for Bert had spoken rather loudly.

"Oh, Bert, it's you, is it?" asked Dr. Martin, for he knew the Bobbsey twins. "What's the trouble at your house?"

Bert told him, mentioning that his father

and mother, as well as Sam and Dinah, were away.

"And you twins are keeping house all alone, are you?" asked the doctor.

"Sure we are," said Bert, a bit proudly.

"Well, you're a fine family of children, I'll say that for you!" said Dr. Martin admiringly. "I'll come over and see what I can do for Aunt Sallie in a little while."

"Bring something for the lumbago," advised Bert.

"Yes, I'll do that," the doctor promised, laughing. "And don't get stuck in a snow-drift going back, Bert."

"I won't," said the boy. "But I was stuck in one early this morning," and he told about having fallen off the roof.

Out again into the storm stepped Bert Bobbsey. Back over the way he had come he floundered again. When a little way from home he heard a faint mewing sound.

"It's a cat!" cried Bert. "I wonder if that could be our cat Snoop come back?" For Snoop, with Snap, the dog, had been sent away to an animal doctor's for a time. The mewing of the cat sounded more plainly, and Bert looked around.

Then, up in a tree, but not far above the ground, he saw a little maltese kitten.

"Oh, you poor little cat!" exclaimed Bert. "I guess you're lost in the storm. I'll take you home."

He reached up, and, by standing on his tiptoes, managed to get hold of the pussy. She dug her claws into the bark of the tree, for she was afraid of falling. But Bert gently pulled her loose, and then cuddled her in his arms, murmuring:

"Oh, you're a nice little kitten! I'm glad I found you! Flossie and Freddie will just love you and Nan will give you some warm milk. I guess you got out of some house and don't know how to get back."

However, there were no houses very near the tree in which Bert had found the little cat. So, not knowing to whom she belonged, he took her home with him. At first the pussy mewed pitifully as Bert cuddled her in his arms. But soon she began to purr contentedly

"Now you're happy," said the boy.

Nan opened the side door for Bert, for she was watching for him to come back, and at first she did not see the cat.

"Is the doctor coming?" Nan wanted to know.

"He'll be here in a little while," was the answer.

Then the pussy in Bert's arms moved and Nan caught sight of the bright eyes and the little tail waving.

"Oh, the darling!" she cried. "Where did you get her, Bert?"

"Found her mewing up in a tree."

By this time Flossie and Freddie, having heard Bert enter, ran to greet him, and they, too, saw the pussy.

"Oh, can I have her?" Flossie wanted to know, reaching up to stroke the animal in Bert's arms.

"Is that Snoop growed little?" Freddie asked, for Snoop was a very big cat.

"This is Snowflake—a new cat," Bert answered. "I named her Snowflake because I got her out in the snowstorm."

"Oh, I just love her!" cried Flossie. "Please let me hold Snowflake!"

"I want to hold her, too," broke in Freddie.

"Now look here!" said Bert, somewhat sternly. "There must be no pulling this pussy apart by you two to see who's going to hold her. You must take turns. As soon as I hear you disputing over the pussy I'll put her back in the tree where I found her."

This was such a terrible thing to think of having happen that Flossie and Freddie were quite alarmed.

"I won't pull the pussy," promised Freddie.

"And I won't, either," said Flossie. "Freddie, you can take her now for a little while, if you like. And I'll take a turn afterward."

"All right, Flossie, thank you," said Freddie politely.

Very gently he took the pussy in his arms, and Nan and Bert looked at each other, smiling over the heads of the smaller Bobbsey children.

"It's a good thing you said that to them, or else they'd be disputing all the while," whispered Nan. "Now they'll be quiet for a time."

Dr. Martin came in a little while and went up to see Mrs. Pry.

"Where does it hurt you the most?" he asked the old lady.

"What's that?" cried Aunt Sallie, sitting up in bed. "You say you fell over a post? I hope you didn't get hurt, Dr. Martin."

"No, I didn't fall over a post," said the doctor, and then he looked up to see Nan behind Mrs. Pry's back motioning to her ears, to let him know the old lady was deaf. "I asked you where the pain hurt *most?*"

"Oh, the pain—yes. You don't speak as loudly as you used to, Dr. Martin, or else my hearing is getting bad. Why, the pain mostly is in my back."

The doctor then asked her other questions and left some medicine for her, saying he thought she would be better in a few days.

"Keep her warm," he told Nan, as he was leaving, having promised to come the next day. "Heat is the best thing for lumbago."

"I've been giving her hot flatirons for her back," Nan explained.

"That's a good idea—keep it up," said Dr. Martin. "And how are you getting on with your housekeeping, alone as you are?"

"Oh, pretty well," Nan said. "Of course we're lonesome without father and mother. And when the window got smashed early this morning we were all frightened. But Bert fixed it."

"Yes, and he nearly fixed himself at the same time," laughed the doctor as he remembered what Bert had told him about falling off the porch roof. "Well, good-bye and good luck," he said, as he went out into the storm. "And keep Aunt Sallie warm."

Nan felt better, now that the doctor had called, and she was glad Flossie and Freddie had the kitten to play with. But soon Freddie came to Nan in the kitchen and said:

"Snowflake is hungry. She wants some milk, I guess."

"We haven't any milk, except sweetened condensed, and I don't believe she'll like that," Nan said. "I wish we had some fresh milk and some other things from the store."

"I'll go," offered Bert. "It isn't snowing quite so hard now."

This was true. The flakes were not falling quite so fast and the wind had gone down a little. So Nan thought it would be all right for Bert to venture out. Freddie, of course, wanted to go, but it was not hard to persuade him to stay in to help Flossie look after Snowflake.

Nan told Bert what to buy at the store and gave him a basket in which to carry the groceries.

"I'll stop at the post-office and see if there's any mail in yet," decided the Bobbsey boy as once more he went out into the snow.

He went to the post-office first, and was much disappointed when he learned that there were no letters for him or Nan.

"The trains snowed up yet?" asked Bert.

"Most of them must be," said the postmaster. "Anyhow, no mail has come in. Maybe there'll be some to-morrow."

Bert certainly hoped so, and he could not help worrying about his father and mother.

They might be in a train that was buried deep in a great heap of snow, and there might be nothing to eat in the cars.

"I wish they'd come home," sighed Bert.

He found several men and boys in the store, buying things to eat, for it had not been possible to make any deliveries. Charlie Mason was there, getting things for his folks.

"Say, it's fun, not to have to go to school, isn't it?" asked Charlie.

"Yes, some fun," Bert admitted. "But I guess it will open in a few days now. This storm can't last much longer."

"No, I guess not," answered Charlie. "Seen anything of Danny Rugg?"

"Yes, I saw him the other day," Bert answered. "But I don't like him any more."

"Nor I," agreed Charlie. "Danny is getting bad again—like he used to be."

The two boys parted outside the store, Charlie going one way with his basket of food, and Bert the other. And it was when Bert came in front of the church—the same church where the window had been broken—that Bert once more saw Danny Rugg.

This time the young bully did not see Bert, for Danny was intent on slipping in the side door of the church, which was open. Danny also had a basket of food.

"Say, this is queer!" murmured Bert to himself. "What's he going into the church again for? I'm going to find out. Maybe he's going to try to mend that broken window," and Bert looked up at the stained glass. It had not yet been repaired, a plain piece of white glass having been put over the hole.

Waiting a moment, until Danny was inside the church, Bert softly followed. He set his basket of groceries down in the vestibule, stood still and listened.

He heard Danny tramping up to the balcony.

"Now I'll catch him at whatever he's up to," whispered Bert to himself. "And I'm not going to fall down any trapdoors, either!"

CHAPTER XX

DANNY'S RING

BERT knew that he must be very careful and cautious this time. Not only must he watch out for the open trapdoor, but he must take care that Danny neither saw nor heard him.

"For if he hears me," said Bert to himself, "he'll run out and then I can't find why he came in here. Danny's smart, but I've got to be smarter."

Moving slowly across the vestibule floor and looking back to see that his basket of groceries was safe, Bert soon reached a place where he knew the trapdoor to be.

"It's closed," he told himself. "That's good! No danger now of falling down. And I hope nobody else comes in here. They might take the things in my basket, and Nan and the others would go hungry. But I guess

226

I'd have to go back to the store and get more," silently chuckled Bert.

Having made sure that the trapdoor, down which he had fallen on his previous visit to the church, was closed, Bert stood near it for a while and listened. He could hear Danny moving about "upstairs," as you might call it, though really it was in the gallery of the church.

This gallery held the big pipe organ, which made such thunderous music on Sundays, and in this gallery the choir singers also had their places.

The remainder of the balcony was given over to pews for the congregation to sit in, when the pews on the main floor of the church were filled. The boys always liked to sit up in the balcony, for they seemed off by themselves when they did this. But the ushers and some of the deacons did not like the boys to go to the gallery, for fear the lads would "cut up." And sometimes this very thing happened. And you may easily guess that Danny Rugg was among the "cut-ups."

"Maybe that's the reason he's going up

there now," thought Bert to himself. "Maybe he's getting ready to play some trick in church next Sunday—he and Sam Todd. He couldn't be coming up to mend the broken window. He wouldn't know how to put in all the different pieces of colored glass, and, anyhow, he didn't have any glass with him ,when he came in here."

Bert's thought that Danny might be preparing for some trick to be played in church the following Sunday came about because once before, about a year ago, Danny and Sam had hidden a little dog up in the gallery one Saturday night. And the following Sunday, when the minister was preaching, the dog crawled out from beneath a pew, walked downstairs and up the middle aisle of the church, much to the amusement of Danny and his cronies.

But the deacons and the minister did not like this, for it disturbed the congregation, and of course it was a wrong thing for Danny to have done.

Because of that trick, the boys had been forbidden to go up in the gallery unless their parents were with them. All this Bert thought of as he stood in the silent church, trying to find out what it was that Danny had come in about.

"I'll follow after him as easy as I can," said Bert to himself. "Maybe I can watch him. But I mustn't let him see me."

Bert wore his rubber boots. So, for that matter, did Danny Rugg, for the snow was so deep that boots were needed. But Bert walked more softly in his boots than did Danny, who tramped around in the balcony as if he did not care who heard him. Bert went on his tiptoes, and the rubber soles of his boots made very little noise.

Up the balcony stairs the Bobbsey boy followed the other lad. It was very still and quiet in the church, and the footsteps of Danny echoed with a strange, hollow sound. On account of the snow covering the ground outside there was no noise of rattling wagons or trucks, so the church was even more quiet than usual.

How different it was from Sundays, when the people were coming in or going out, when the place was lighted, and when there was organ music and singing.

"I don't like church on week days," thought Bert.

But he had come in for a special purpose, and he was going to carry it out. Step after step he went up to the gallery floor, making no noise. He could still hear Danny moving about.

. At last Bert reached a place where, in the dim light that came through the stained-glass window, he could see Danny walking along between the rows of pews.

"He's right near the broken window," whispered Bert to himself. "And he's looking on the floor for something. I wonder what it is? He can't be looking for the broken bits of stained glass, to put them back —they were picked up long ago. I wonder what it is he's looking for?"

Danny was certainly looking for something. He bent over and let his eyes rove about the floor, right under the window that had been broken. Closely and carefully Danny searched.

Then, almost as if some one had shouted it at him, there came into Bert's mind the thought:

"Danny's looking for his lost birthday ring! It must have slipped off his finger in one of the snowballs he threw that day of the first storm. The gold ring stuck in the snow-ball, and Danny threw the snowball at the window! The ball broke the glass and came inside the balcony here. And Danny must know that! He hasn't found his ring any-where else, and he knows it must have been in that snowball!"

The idea excited Bert and made his heart beat faster.

"When the snowball melted," thought Bert, still watching Danny eagerly, "the ring would drop out on the floor and stay there. It's his ring that Danny's searching for!"

Bert grew so excited at this thought that he made a sudden movement. His foot slipped and banged against a pew.

"What's that?" cried Danny, jumping up. "Who's there?"

Bert was quick enough to dodge down behind one of the pews, so that when Danny looked up he saw no one.

But though Danny saw no one, he was frightened because of the noise, and, not stopping any longer to search for his lost ring, or whatever it was he was looking for, he darted out of the balcony and down the stairs, with many a clatter of his rubber boots.

"Say, he's running like a scared rabbit!" chuckled Bert to himself. "I wish I dared yell at him, so he'd know who it is that's looking at him. But I guess I'd better not. I want to see if his ring is here."

Pausing not to look back, Danny ran down to the main floor and out of the side door.

"I hope he doesn't take my basket of groceries," thought Bert. But he remembered he had set it over in a dark corner, where it would not be likely to be seen. And, as a matter of fact, Danny Rugg was so frightened that he thought of nothing but taking his own basket of food and hurrying out of the church.

Bert heard the door slam after the other

boy, and then the Bobbsey lad began to wonder what was the best thing to do.

"If Danny's ring is there and I find it, I can prove that he threw the snowball that broke the window," said Bert to himself. "But even if I pick up the ring on the balcony floor, Danny might say I found it somewhere else and put it there. I ought to have some one with me when I find it—if I do—and whoever's with me can say I didn't put it there. I've got to get some one to help me."

Bert remembered that Mr. Henry Ander, one of the church deacons, a good and kindly man who was well acquainted with the Bobbsey family, lived close to the church.

"I'll go and get Mr. Ander before I look for the ring," decided Bert.

He started down the balcony stairs, though he was more than anxious to look for the lost ring, for the finding of that would clear Bert's name from the suspicion of having broken the window. But knowing that the plan he had made was best, Bert kept on.

As he was crossing the dim vestibule on his

way to the side door, Bert heard some one coming in.

"I hope that isn't Danny coming back!" Bert whispered.

It was not. It was Mr. Shull.

"Well, Bert, what in the world are you doing here?" asked the sexton, in surprise. "Are you trying to fall down the trapdoor again?"

"No, sir," answered the boy.

"You couldn't, very well, anyhow," went on the janitor. "For the door is closed."

"I didn't come in here for that," said Bert. "Listen, Mr. Shull. Do you remember when the church window was broken?"

"I should say I do remember it, Bert! They said you did it, but I have my doubts of that."

"I didn't do it," said Bert. "But I know who did. It was Danny Rugg, and I can prove it if I can find his gold ring on the floor. It was in the snowball he threw, and Danny was in here just now, trying to find his ring."

Bert told all that had happened.

"I want to get Mr. Ander," went on the

Bobbsey boy. "If he and you see me find the ring, you'll know I didn't throw that snowball."

"It's a good idea, Bert!" exclaimed the sexton. "Go get the deacon, and we'll look for the ring together—all three of us."

Mr. Ander was surprised a few minutes later when Bert, much excited, poured out the story of the snowball, the broken window, and the lost ring.

"All right, Bert," he said at length. "I'll go with you and look for the ring. And if we find it, I'll take it and give it to Mr. Rugg with Danny there looking on. And I'll take you with me. We'll clear you of the charge of having broken the window."

A little later the eager, excited boy and the two men, almost as eager as Bert himself, were looking over the floor beneath the broken window. The sexton got his electric flashlight and the sharp beams of this glinted over the floor.

"Look! I see something glittering like gold!" cried Bert, pointing to a crack under a pew. "See if that's the ring!"

The sexton focused his light on the object. Mr. Ander took out his knife, and with the blade of it pried the shining object out of the crack.

"It's a gold ring, all right," he said, holding it up to the light.

"See if it has any initials on it," suggested Bert.

"Hold the light closer, Mr. Shull," said the deacon. When this had been done he slowly said: "It's got the letters D. R. on it—this ring has."

"Then it's Danny Rugg's ring!" cried Bert. "It was in the snowball that broke the window. That's what he was up here looking for! Oh, I'm so glad we've found it!"

CHAPTER XXI

FIRE

The deacon, Mr. Ander, and the sexton looked carefully around on the floor of the balcony near the broken window. They even found some little slivers of colored glass, for only the larger pieces had been swept up.

"Danny's ring certainly came in here, stuck to the snowball he threw against the window," decided the deacon. "It's as plain as if we saw it happen. And I think, Bert, when I hand this ring to Danny's father and tell how it was found—I think Danny will confess just how it happened. I want you with me when he does, so your name will be cleared."

"Yes, I'd like to go with you," Bert said. "But I ought to go home now. I've been away a good while, and maybe Nan might want some of the groceries I have in the basket downstairs. Nan is home alone with

Flossie and Freddie. Mrs. Pry is sick in bed."

"Then you'd better go home now," agreed the deacon when Bert had further explained how it was the Bobbsey twins were keeping house by themselves. "This evening after supper I'll call for you and we'll take this ring back to Danny."

"Do you want me to come along?" asked the sexton. "I'm going to be pretty busy, keeping up the fires, for it's going to be a cold night."

"Yes, it is," agreed Mr. Ander. "No, I don't believe we need you, Robert. Two witnesses are enough to prove where the lost ring was found."

"All right," agreed Bert. "I'll be ready for you after supper."

It was with a very much lighter heart than he had had on entering the church that Bert left the edifice. Picking up his basket of groceries he started for home.

"Say, it is mighty cold!" he murmured as he felt the tingling air nip his ears and nose. "I'll have to keep up a good fire in our furnace. Mrs. Pry has got to be kept warm with her lumbago."

On leaving the church, Bert looked around for a sight of Danny Rugg, but that small bully and cheat was not in view, and Bert was glad of it.

"For if he saw me coming out of the church," reasoned Bert," he would guess that I made the noise that scared him away. Now he'll be surprised when we hand him his ring."

Mr. Ander put the gold finger ornament in his pocket and went back home, planning to go to Bert's house in the evening. Danny lived not far from the Bobbsey house.

"I'm glad it can be proved that Bert didn't break the window," said the sexton.

"So am I," agreed the deacon. "Bert's a good boy. I never liked to think that he broke the window. Yet the other boys said he did."

"Well, Danny never actually said so," remarked Mr. Shull. "But he kept quiet about it when he knew that he, himself, had thrown the snowball that did the damage. It was just as bad as if Danny had said Bert did it."

"Just the same," agreed the deacon.

Bert found Nan and the small twins waiting rather anxiously for him when he got back.

"Did you get a letter from mother?" asked Nan as soon as the door was opened.

"No, not yet."

"Oh, dear! I wonder what's the matter," and tears were in Nan's eyes.

"They're all right," declared Bert. "It's just that the mails are late on account of the storm. I guess we'll hear from them by to-morrow. But, Nan, I've got good news."

"What is it?" she asked. "Did you see Sam and Dinah coming back?"

"No. But maybe they'll be along soon. But I found Danny's ring in the church under the broken window, and that proves he did it," and the boy quickly told his sister what had happened.

"Oh, I'm glad of that!" cried Nan. "Danny was mean to keep still and let it be thought you did it."

"Yes, he's a sort of a sneak," agreed Bert.

"But wait until he sees the deacon and me with his ring! He'll feel queer then!"

Flossie and Freddie were playing about the house when Bert came back, and they were delighted when he gave them some sticks of candy he had bought at the store.

"Aunt Sallie says she feels cold," reported Nan, when she had taken a cup of tea and one of the lamb chops Bert had brought up to the invalid. "Can you make the house any warmer, Bert? You know Doctor Martin said we must keep her lumbago warm."

"I'll turn on the furnace more, shake it down and put a lot of coal on," decided the boy. "I'm glad we have plenty of coal in the bin."

"So am I!" agreed Nan.

Soon the pipes were cracking with the additional heat that Bert turned on. And though the wind still blew cold outside and though more flakes of snow began to fall as evening settled down, the Bobbsey twins were warm and snug.

Of course they were lonesome without their parents, and they surely wished Dinah and

Sam would return. But Bert and Nan, putting aside their own feelings, amused Flossie and Freddie, so that the small twins laughed merrily.

"Will you be afraid to stay here while I go out with Mr. Ander a little while?" asked Bert of his sister, when supper was over.

"Oh, no," Nan answered. "That is, if you don't stay too late."

"I won't," he promised. "Only long enough to give Danny back his ring and see what he has to say."

A little later the deacon arrived at the Bobbsey house. He went to the side door and brushed the snow off his boots with a broom that was kept there for the purpose.

"Is it snowing much?" asked Bert, as he let Mr. Ander in.

"Yes, snowing hard," was the answer. "I don't know when we've had so much snow this early in the winter. It keeps up as if it would never stop. How are you, Nan?" he asked kindly. "And how is the fat fairy and the big fireman?" he asked, patting Flossie and Freddie.

Fairy and fireman were the pet names Mr. Bobbsey often called his small twins, and the deacon, being a friend of the family, remembered this.

"I'm all right," Freddie answered. "Do you think there'll be a fire to-night, Mr. Deacon?"

"Mr. Ander—not Mr. Deacon!" corrected Nan.

"Oh, it's all the same," laughed the kindly man. "Names don't mean anything. But I surely hope there won't be any fires, little man. The engines would have hard work getting through the drifts."

"We got a little kittie out of a snowdrift," said Flossie. "Bert found her and she's named Snowflake. Here she is," and she picked up the little cat and put her in the deacon's lap.

"Say, she's real cute!" laughed Mr. Ander, who was fond of animals. He gently rubbed the pussy's ears and scratched her under her chin, which she seemed to like very much.

By this time Bert was dressed to go out and he and the deacon started through the storm to the Rugg home, not far away. Mr. Rugg, who opened the door, seemed surprised to meet Bert and Mr. Ander.

"Good evening," greeted the deacon. "Is Danny in?"

"Danny? Yes, I guess so," answered Mr. Rugg slowly. "Did you want to see him? Has he been doing anything?"

"Oh, nothing new. And it isn't such a terrible thing, after all, I suppose," replied the deacon. "The worst part of it was keeping quiet and letting some one else be blamed. Oh, there you are, Danny," he went on, as the boy himself came into the room.

No sooner did Danny catch sight of Bert and the deacon than he seemed to know what was "in the wind," as the saying is.

Mr. Ander lost no time.

"Is this your ring, Danny?" asked the deacon, holding out on the palm of his hand the gold circlet.

Before Danny could answer Mr. Rugg stepped forward and took the ring from the deacon.

"Why, yes, that's Danny's ring!" exclaimed the boy's father. "I bought it for his birthday. He told me he lost it at school. I guess he did, for only yesterday I met the principal and he said the ring hadn't been found."

"Well, it's found now," said Mr. Ander, with a little smile at Bert. "And though Danny didn't exactly lose it at school, it was near there. That's your ring, isn't it, Danny?" he asked.

"Yes—yes, sir," faltered the boy. "It's my birthday ring."

"Don't you want to know where we found it—where Bert and I found it?" went on the deacon.

"Yes—yes, sir, I—I guess I do." Danny's voice was low.

"Maybe you can guess where we found it," went on the deacon, while Mr. Rugg looked curiously at his son and then at the visitors. "I think you can guess, Danny, but I'm going to tell you.

"Bert and I and Mr. Shull, the sexton.

found your ring in the church balcony, right under the broken stained-glass window. The window was broken by a snowball thrown through it, Danny. The ring must have been in the snowball, and when the snow melted the ring fell out on the floor and into a crack. It has been there ever since. Danny Rugg, were you in the church this afternoon looking for this lost ring?"

The deacon's voice was now stern.

Danny hung his head.

"Answer, Danny," ordered his father. "Is this true?"

"Yes—yes, sir," mumbled Danny. "I went there to look for my ring. I—I thought it might have been in the snowball."

"Did you throw the snowball that broke the church window?" asked Mr. Rugg in stern tones.

Danny hung his head and was silent.

"Better own up and tell the truth," said the deacon more gently.

"Oh, I did it! Yes, I did it!" and Danny burst out crying. "I didn't mean to, but I broke the window. I was trying to throw over the church, but my hand slipped and the ball went through the window.

"Then, right after that, I missed my ring. First I thought it had dropped off. But when it wasn't found I thought maybe it had stuck to the snowball and gone inside the church. So I went in to look.

"I went in once before, but I heard a noise and I ran out. That was when Bert fell down the trapdoor."

"Is that so, Bert?" asked the deacon.

"Yes, sir," was the answer. "I didn't want to say why I went in the church, though, until I could be sure what Danny wanted in there."

"And you went into the church the second time, to-day, Danny, did you?" asked the deacon.

"Yes, sir. I went to see if I could find my ring. And if I found it I was going to tell that I broke the window—and that it wasn't Bert."

"Better late than never," the deacon said. "Well, I guess Bert is cleared now."

"Yes, I'll tell everything," sobbed Danny. "I wouldn't have let it be thought Bert did it, only Sam said he saw Bert throw the same time I did, and I thought, maybe, after all, Bert's ball broke the glass."

"It didn't!" exclaimed Bert. "For I only threw my snowball on the ground."

Mr. Rugg placed the ring on the table. Danny was still sobbing brokenly in one corner of the room.

"I am very sorry this has happened," said Mr. Rugg. "I will punish Danny for his part in it, and I will pay for the broken window, Mr. Ander. I will also make Danny get up in front of the whole school and confess so Bert's name will be cleared."

"If you do that and the window is paid for, I think Danny will have been punished enough," suggested the deacon. "I don't believe he will ever do a thing like this again. Will you, Danny?"

"Oh, no, never! Never! Not as long as I live!" sobbed the boy, and Bert felt sorry for him.

"Well, this is what we came for, and I'm glad it's over with," announced Mr. Ander. "I'll trust you to pay for the stained-glass window, Mr. Rugg, and also see to it that Danny tells the truth as soon as school opens again."

"I'll take care of it," promised Danny's father.

Bert waited a moment and then walked over to where his former chum was standing, sobbing.

"It's all right, Danny," said Bert in a low voice. "I don't mind, now that it's known I didn't do it. I'll be friends with you again."

"Tha-thanks," faltered Danny, and then the hands of the two boys met in a firm clasp.

"They'll be better friends than ever," whispered the deacon to Mr. Rugg.

"I hope so," said the father. "Danny needs a lesson. I hope he will profit by this one."

Nan rejoiced with Bert when he got home and told all that had happened. The smaller twins had gone to bed, the "sandman" having paid them an early visit.

Nan went up to see if Mrs. Pry wanted anything, and gave her some of the medicine the doctor had left for her.

"It's snowing yet," Nan said to the old lady.

"What's that? You say the kitten's got a fit?" cried Mrs. Pry. "Land sakes! Well, put it down the cellar!"

"No, no! The kitten hasn't a fit! I said it was snowing *yet!*" said Nan loudly.

"Oh! More snow! Seems like it was never going to stop! I do hope the house keeps warm, for my pains seem to be getting worse."

Nan was more lonesome than ever that night, wished more for her father and mother, but she said nothing to Bert about it. She was the first up the next morning, and she felt a sense of chill as she moved about dressing.

"Bert! Bert!" she softly called to her brother, so as not to awaken Flossie and Freddie. "I'm afraid the fire has gone out, Bert, or else it's very low. You'd better look after it."

"I will," said Bert sleepily as he got out of bed and hastily dressed to go down cellar. As Nan put the coffee on to boil, so Mrs. Pry

could have an early, hot cup, the girl heard
her brother rattling away at the furnace.

"Fire's out," he called up. "But I'll soon
have it going again."

He piled in wood and lighted the paper,
and then, after putting on some coal, came
upstairs.

"It will soon be warm," he said.

"I hope so!" exclaimed Nan, shivering as
she set the table for breakfast.

Flossie and Freddie were just awakening
when Nan carried up Mrs. Pry some toast
and coffee and an egg. The old lady sat up
in bed and suddenly exclaimed:

"Nan, I smell smoke!"

"I guess it's the toast," Nan answered.
"One slice burned a little."

"No, it isn't toast!" insisted Aunt Sallie.
"I know the smell of burned toast! This is
burning wood! I hope the chimney isn't on
fire."

"Oh, no, I guess it isn't," replied Nan.
"Bert just made up a new fire in the
furnace."

Just then Freddie cried:

"Oh, look at the smoke! There's a lot of smoke out in the hall!"

Nan looked out of Mrs. Pry's room. Truly the hall was filling with a blue, choking haze.

"It's a fire!" screamed Flossie. "Bert! Nan! The house is on fire!"

More smoke welled up until Nan and the small twins were choking and gasping.

"Bert! Bert!" shouted Nan, running down the stairs. "What is the matter? Is the house on fire?"

CHAPTER XXII

JUST IN TIME

BERT BOBBSEY, who had gone out to clear some of the snow from the side porch, hurried back into the house just as Nan called to him. He, also, saw and smelled the smoke. And he heard the cries of fire, not only shouted by Flossie and Freddie, but also by Mrs. Pry.

The old lady in her excitement, and in spite of the pain in her back, had gotten out of bed and was hurrying around the room, gathering up such of her things as she could find.

"Bert! Bert!" cried Nan again. "What is it? Is the house on fire?"

Much as he feared to admit this, Bert began to think it was what had, most unfortunately, happened.

"Guess I made too much of a blaze in the furnace!" gasped the boy.

Nan saw Bert rushing for the door leading to the cellar.

"Don't go down there!" she cried.

"I've got to! That's where the fire has started!" he called back. "I'll see if I can't put it out before it gets any worse."

"No! No!" shouted Nan. "You'll get burned. If the house is on fire we must telephone in an alarm. Mother always said to call the engines first thing! Telephone in the alarm, Bert!"

"I can't telephone the alarm in, Nan," he said.

"Why not?"

"The telephone's broken! I'll have to run down the street and pull the box!"

"Can't you go next door and telephone?" Nan wanted to know. "Oh, of course you can't! Oh, it's getting worse, Bert!"

It surely was—at least the smoke was.

"Get Flossie and Freddie out!" gasped the boy. "And Aunt Sallie! Never mind the house—let it burn!"

"Oh, Bert Bobbsey! Let our lovely house burn!"

"Well, we can't put it out, can we? Get Flossie and Freddie out and Mrs. Pry! I'll go pull the fire box!"

It seemed the best thing to do. Upstairs ran Nan to the playroom where Flossie and Freddie were crying, for they were much frightened.

"Come!" called Nan. "We must get out! The house is burning!"

"I'm going to take my dolls!" exclaimed Flossie, catching two or three of her most cherished ones in her arms.

"And I'm going to take my fire engine!" shouted Freddie. "If it was a bigger one, maybe it could put out the fire."

"Don't stop to pick up any of your toys!" ordered Nan. "But come with me!"

She caught the children, each by an arm, and fairly pulled them out into the hall. At the same time she cried:

"Can you get down, Aunt Sallie? The house is on fire!"

"No need to tell me that!" cried the old

lady, who seemed suddenly to forget about her aches and pains. "I can smell smoke, even if I am a little deaf!"

She hobbled out into the hall, having slipped a warm bathrobe on. In one hand she carried her shoes, and in the other her half-filled valise, while under her arms she had bundles of her clothing.

"Land sakes, this is terrible! Driven out in the middle of winter!" she cried.

As Bert opened the front door to rush down the street to the nearest fire box he almost fell off the porch in his excitement, for, rushing up the front walk was—his father!

And behind him came Mrs. Bobbsey!

"Bert! Bert!" cried his father, seeing the smoke. "What has happened?"

"House on fire!" shouted Bert. "I'm going to turn in the alarm! Telephone's broke!"

As he swung out of the gate Bert was given a further surprise by colliding with Sam Johnson, who dropped the valise he was carrying.

"Fo' de lan' sakes!" gasped Sam.

The breath was almost knocked out of Bert, but he had a vision of fat Dinah waddling up the street. At first Bert thought it was all a dream—his father and mother and Sam and Dinah all coming home at once and so unexpectedly! But he was soon sure it was no dream, and certainly the smoke pouring out of the front door was real enough.

"Oh, Sam! The house is on fire!" cried Mrs. Bobbsey. "Where are the children? Nan! Flossie! Freddie! And where's Mrs. Pry?"

"They're coming out!" cried Bert. "You look after them. I'll get the engines!"

"Don't get de engines!" shouted Sam. "Don't!"

"But the house is on fire!" exclaimed Mr. Bobbsey.

"No it ain't!" insisted Sam. "I know whut it is. I kin tell by de smell ob de smoke. It's de furnace in de cellar. Did you put on wood, Bert?"

"Yes, I just made a new fire!"

"It's de furnace all right," said Sam. "You done got de damper turned de wrong way.

It happened to me once. It's gwine to be aw right in a minute. De house ain't on fire. It's jest de furnace. I'll fix her!"

He dashed into the house and down the cellar steps. By this time Nan, with the smaller twins and Aunt Sallie, reached the front steps.

In spite of the cold, a crowd was gathering in the street, attracted by the smoke, and several men offered to turn in an alarm, but Mr. Bobbsey told them to wait. In a minute or two Sam came out again, his eyes running with tears on account of the smoke.

"Dat's just whut I t'ought it was," he gasped. "Damper turned de wrong way. De furnace has stopped smokin' now, an' I opened a lot of windows. We kin go back in de house soon."

In a little while, they could do so. With the damper properly turned, the smoke from the new fire in the furnace went up the chimney, as it should, and through the open windows the smoke in the house soon blew out.

"Well, my poor dears, what a fright you must have had!" said Mrs. Bobbsey, holding Flossie and Freddie on her lap while Bert and

Nan stood near. "And all alone too! We didn't know until a little while ago that Sam and Dinah were away. But I suppose Mrs. Pry looked after you."

"No, I'm sorry to say, I couldn't," said Mrs. Pry, who had by this time put on a few clothes. "I was taken with the lumbago soon after Dinah went away, and these children have been keeping house by themselves. And very well they did it, too!"

"You ought to get back in bed, Aunt Sallie, with your lumbago!" said Nan. "The doctor said we must keep you warm."

"Yes, he did, my dear," said Aunt Sallie, with a smile. "But I never thought, and I don't believe he did, either, that you'd make me think the house was on fire to keep me warm. But I don't seem to have any lumbago left. I feel much better. I guess the fright cured me."

And so it seemed, for Aunt Sallie moved about as well as before she had had to go to bed.

The Bobbsey twins got over their fright, and the crowd, which had feared the Bobb-

sey house was burning, moved away. Sam
made the fire good and hot, without letting
it smoke. The house was soon put to rights
again. And once more there were happy,
smiling faces.

"But we didn't know you were coming
home," said Nan to her mother. "Is Uncle
Rossiter better?"

"Yes, he's all right. We sent you word
that we were coming, but I guess you didn't
get any mail. We had none from you."

"The storm was too bad," stated Bert.
"And didn't you know Sam had to go away
and then Dinah had to go after Sam?"

"No, we didn't know a thing about it," said
Mr. Bobbsey. "Coming home on the train
we saw Sam and Dinah get on at the junction
early this morning, and that was the first we
knew they had had to leave."

Dinah explained that she had found Sam
not as sick as at first reported, and she soon
had him "on his feet again," as she called it.
His brother, too, got better, so there was no
need of Sam's remaining in the South, and

the two faithful servants hurried back as soon as they could.

"Oh, I'm so glad you're all back!" exclaimed Nan. "It's been hard work, keeping house alone."

"It must have been, my dear," said her mother. "You were brave children. So many things must have happened."

"There did," sighed Nan.

"I sat in the biksits!" laughed Flossie.

"And Bert fell off the roof!" said Freddie.

"And the window's broke!" added Flossie.

Then all the happenings were told, including how Bert found Danny's ring in the church.

A few days after that the weather cleared and it grew warmer. School resumed, and one of the first things done was to make Danny Rugg get up in front of all the classes and tell that he had broken the window. Thus was Bert's name cleared and Sam Todd was made to apologize to him.

"Well, I'm glad this is over," said the principal. "I congratulate you, Bert Bobbsey!"

And Bert felt very happy.

"Well, I guess you don't need me any more," said Mrs. Pry a few days later.

"But we hope you'll come and see us some other time," said Mrs. Bobbsey.

"What's that?" exclaimed Aunt Sallie. "Is the kitten hanging on the line?"

When it was explained to her what Mrs. Bobbsey had said, Aunt Sallie joined in laughing at her mistake.

And now that we can leave them happy and contented, we shall say good-bye to the children until we meet them again. An interesting vacation was to come to them soon, to be called, "The Bobbsey Twins at Clover Bank."

As Daddy Bobbsey was leaving for work one morning he smiled to himself, for he had just heard this conversation:

"Let's play house!" Freddie had suggested.

"I'll be Aunt Sallie," shouted Flossie.

"We'll not sit in biscuits!" laughed Nan.

"Nor have a fire!" added Bert.

THE END